FOLK TALES FROM THE NORTH

FOLK TALES FROM THE NORTH

By Winifred Finlay

Illustrated by Victor Ambrus

FRANKLIN WATTS INC.
575 Lexington Ave., New York, N.Y. 10022

First published by
KAYE & WARD LIMITED
194-200 Bishopsgate, London, E.C.2
1968

First American publication, 1969, by Franklin Watts, Inc.

Library of Congress Catalog Card Number: 69–10886

Printed in Great Britain

CONTENTS

The following stories have been previously published in *Child Education*: The Laidley Worm of Spindlestone Heugh, The Ji-jaller Bag, Mary-Ann and the Cauld Lad of Hylton, Jonas and the Boggart of Brixworth.

ILLUSTRATIONS

For Gill and David, with love

I

JIP AND THE WITCH OF WALGRAVE

Once upon a time, in a pleasant wood on the outskirts of the village of Walgrave in Northamptonshire, there lived an elf and a witch.

The witch, who was called Dame Howlett, lived on the northern fringe of the wood in a tumble-down cottage with a thatched roof; she kept a black cat called Blackmalkin who did all the work and received only kicks and blows for his pains; because she was mean, cruel and bad-tempered, everyone in Walgrave feared her and did their best to keep out of her way.

The elf, who was called Jip, lived by himself on the southern fringe of the wood in an oak tree which was more than two hundred years old. He was a lively little fellow with a merry face, sparkling green eyes and yellow hair, and he wore a suit of Lincoln green to match his eyes and a red, pointed cap on his yellow hair.

If you were to ask whether he was a good elf or a bad one, it would be very difficult for me to give you an answer. Some days he would wake up feeling kind and helpful so that he would put a spell on the axe of Will the Woodman and the forester would find he was doing twice the work with half the effort, or he would give old Rob the Roadmender the secret good luck sign so that the big stones would break up into fragments before his heavy hammer so much as touched them.

On other days, however, he would feel quite different, and he'd cast a spell on the dairymaid's milk so that it would not turn to butter, or he'd disguise himself as a three-legged stool and then disappear just as the tired farmer sat down on him.

In other words, although Jip was an elf, he was very like any ordinary boy or girl such as I might be talking to at this very minute, and, like the little girl in the nursery rhyme, when he was good he was very, very good, but when he was bad, he was horrid.

Naturally no one liked it when Jip was mischievous and played tricks on them, but they soon got over their anger and everyone —the farmers and their labourers, the village people of Walgrave, Will the Woodman and old Rob the Roadmender and little Jip himself—all lived together more or less happily until the day that Dame Howlett, the wicked old witch, decided that she was tired of her diet of rabbits and nuts and berries and milk stolen from the farmers' cows.

'What I fancy is a nicely roasted elf served on a slice of barley bread,' she said, and then she kicked Blackmalkin.

'Sweep and dust and polish and clean.
An idle cat should never be seen,'

she cried, and she kicked him again and then, picking up the old sack which she used when she gathered the nuts which fell from the oak and the beech and the chestnut and the hazel trees, she set off for the oak which was more than two hundred years old and which was Jip's home, and she knocked three times on the deeply furrowed bark of the massive trunk.

'Pretty little Jip,' she called out in a false, coaxing voice. 'Come and see the sack of cherries I have brought you, so red and so sweet.'

'Sweet red cherries!' Jip cried, flinging open the door in the trunk of the old oak tree and running out excitedly. 'Why, just at this very moment I was sitting in my parlour thinking how nice it would be to be eating sweet red cherries. Where are they, kind Dame Howlett?'

'In my sack,' the old witch answered, opening the mouth of her sack just a very little.

'I can't see any,' Jip said, peering into the darkness.

'Look closer,' the witch urged, and then she gave Jip a sudden push with her skinny hand so that he stumbled right into the sack. 'Aha!' she cried triumphantly, tying a string tightly round the mouth of the sack so that Jip could not escape. 'Take care that the cherry stones do not stick in your throat, my little bird!' Picking up the sack with poor Jip inside, she slung it over her shoulder and set off for her tumble-down cottage at the other end of the wood.

She was just half-way home when it occurred to her that the previous day she had seen some mushrooms growing in Malt Mill Pasture and that mushrooms would go very nicely with roast elf, and so she put the sack down against an elm tree while she went to the field to gather the mushrooms.

At once little Jip began to kick and jump and struggle to escape, but all his efforts were useless: the old witch had tied the string too securely round the mouth of the sack.

'If there was only someone who could help me,' he thought sadly, remembering the times he had helped other people, and then suddenly he heard the sound of a tree being felled, and Jip knew that Will the Woodcutter was working nearby.

'Help!' he cried. 'Will, help me!' But his voice was drowned by the cooing of the ring doves in the topmost branches of the elm tree, and Will continued steadily chopping, chopping, chopping.

'Help!' he cried again. 'Oh, Will, help me!' But his voice was lost in the rustle of dead leaves as a bright-eyed stoat slunk past in search of prey.

'Help!' he cried again. 'Oh, Will, please help me!' And this time Will heard the little voice. Lowering his axe, he stared slowly all around him.

'Surely that's Jip's voice,' he said, scratching his head. 'But where is Jip? Up to his tricks again, I'll be bound.' And he was just going to pick up his axe when Jip called out again.

'It is Jip, and I'm not up to any tricks, Will. Dame Howlett has caught me in her sack and I'm terribly afraid that she means to cook me for her supper.'

'Oh, does she!' said Will, striding over and untying the sack so that Jip bounded out, shivering at his narrow escape, but as soon as he saw the brawny woodcutter and breathed the fresh woodland air, his confidence returned.

'Thank you for helping me, Will,' he cried. 'Now I think I'll fill the sack with brambles and briars so that the old witch won't know I've escaped.'

Will obligingly chopped down some long, prickly brambles and briars and together they filled the sack, tied up its mouth with string, and then Jip ran back to his home in the oak which was more than two hundred years old, while the woodcutter returned to his work.

Presently the old witch returned with her mushrooms, picked up the sack, slung it over her shoulder, and winced as the thorns and prickles stuck into her.

'Who would have thought an elf would have carried a pocketful of pins and needles with him?' she cried. 'Just wait till I get you home, my lad. I'll give you something for sticking them into me like this.'

When she reached her tumble-down cottage she kicked the cat —who had been working hard all day sweeping and dusting and polishing and cleaning and had just that very moment fallen asleep in front of the fire—picked up her broom and beat the sack soundly. When she untied it however and found she had been wasting her strength on a sack of brambles and briars, she was so angry that she did not know what to do with herself, and she would have fallen to beating Blackmalkin had he not slipped out of the open door and hidden himself deep in the heart of the wood.

'So Jip thinks he can trick me, does he?' she muttered. 'Well, we'll soon see about that.'

The next morning she rose early and kicked Blackmalkin.

'Wash and bake and cook and brew
Or else I'll take my broom to you.'

And she kicked him a second time and then, picking up the old sack in which she gathered the nuts which fell from the beech and the sweet chestnut and the hazel trees, she set off for the oak which was more than two hundred years old and which was Jip's home, and she knocked three times on the deeply furrowed bark of the massive trunk.

'Pretty little Jip,' she called out in a false, wheedling voice. 'Come and see the sack of strawberries I have brought you, so tempting and juicy.'

'Tempting, juicy strawberries!' Jip cried, flinging open the door in the trunk of the old oak tree and running out excitedly. 'Why, just at this very moment I was sitting in my kitchen thinking how nice it would be to be eating tempting, juicy strawberries. Where are they, kind Dame Howlett?'

'In my sack,' the old witch answered, opening the mouth of her sack just a very little.

'I can't see any,' Jip said, peering into the darkness.

'Look closer,' the witch urged, and then she gave Jip a sudden push with her skinny hand so that he stumbled right into the sack.

'Aha!' she cried triumphantly, tying a string tightly round the mouth of the sack so that Jip could not escape. 'Take care the juice doesn't choke you, my little bird!' Picking up the sack with poor Jip inside, she slung it over her shoulder and set off for her tumble-down cottage at the other side of the wood.

She was just half-way home when it occurred to her that she had seen the pale purple flowers of sweet marjoram growing near the hedge in Malt Mill Pasture and that sweet marjoram would give a delicate flavour to roast elf, so she put the sack down against a birch tree while she went to the field to pick the herb.

At once little Jip began to kick and jump and struggle to escape,

14

but all his efforts were useless: the old witch had tied the string too securely round the mouth of the sack.

'If there was only someone who could help me,' he thought sadly, remembering the times he had helped other people, and then suddenly he heard the sound of a heavy hammer breaking up stones, and he knew that old Rob the Roadmender was working nearby.

'Help!' he cried. 'Rob, help me!' But his voice was drowned by the loud, echoing laugh of the green woodpecker half-way up the slender birch tree, and Rob continued steadily breaking up his stones.

'Help!' he cried again. 'Oh, Rob, help me!' But his voice was lost in the chattering and scolding of a red squirrel who was frightened by the strange sounds coming from the sack.

'Help!' he cried again. 'Oh, Rob, please help me!' And this time old Rob heard the little voice, and lowering his hammer, he stared slowly all around him.

'Surely that's Jip's voice,' he said, scratching his head. 'But where is Jip? Up to his tricks again, I'll be bound.' And he was just going to pick up his hammer when Jip called out again.

'It is Jip, and I'm not up to any tricks, Rob. Dame Howlett has caught me in her sack and I'm terribly afraid she means to cook me for her supper.'

'Oh, does she, indeed!' said Rob, shuffling over and untying the sack so that Jip bounded out, shivering at his narrow escape, but as soon as he saw the kindly old roadmender and breathed the fresh woodland air, his confidence returned.

'Thank you for helping me, Rob,' he cried. 'Now I think I'll fill the sack with stones so that the old witch won't know I've escaped.'

Rob obligingly carried over some of his stones and together they filled the sack, tied up its mouth with string, and then Jip ran back to his home in the oak which was more than two hundred years old, while the old roadman returned to his work.

Presently the old witch returned with her sweet marjoram, picked up the sack, slung it over her shoulder, and winced at the weight and the sharp edges of the stones which dug into her. 'Who would have thought an elf would have had such sharp, heavy bones?' she cried. 'Just wait till I get you home, my lad. I'll soften your bones for you.'

When she reached her tumble-down cottage she kicked Blackmalkin—who had been working hard all day washing and baking and cooking and brewing and had just that very moment fallen asleep in front of the fire—picked up her broom and beat the sack soundly. When she untied it however and found she had been wasting her strength on a sack of stones, she was so angry that she did not know what to do with herself, and she would have fallen to beating Blackmalkin had he not slipped out of the open door and hidden himself deep in the heart of the wood.

'Twice that cunning Jip has tricked me,' she cried, 'but the third time he will not be so lucky.'

The next morning she rose early and kicked Blackmalkin.

'Patch and darn and mend and sew
Or cold and hungry you will go.'

And she kicked him a second time and went up to her bedroom and disguised herself as an old pedlar-woman, putting on a full black skirt and a grey blouse and shawl and black straw bonnet which almost hid her face. In front of her, and supported by a leather strap which went round the back of her neck, she carried a big wooden box containing pins and needles and brooches, and ribbons and threads and buttons, and pinafores and stockings and one fine pair of scarlet shoes made of the very softest leather.

Instead of going to Jip's home in the old oak tree, the witch lurked in the woods all day until at length she heard the sound of cheerful singing and saw Jip dancing along the path, his suit of Lincoln green matching his eyes and his red, pointed cap on his yellow hair.

16

'Ah, Master Jip!' she cried. 'How merry you sound and how smart you look in your green suit and your red pointed cap. Now I have here just the thing for such a handsome young fellow. What say you to a pair of scarlet shoes to match your scarlet cap, shoes made of the very softest leather?' And she opened the lid of the box she was carrying so that Jip could just catch a glimpse of the pins and needles and brooches, the ribbons and threads and buttons, the pinafores and stockings—AND—the one pair of fine scarlet shoes made of the very softest leather.

'I can't see properly,' Jip said, stretching up on his toes to peer over the edge of the box.

'Jump up on to my tray and inspect the shoes for yourself,' the witch-pedlar-woman said.

Leaping lightly on to the box, Jip picked up the red shoes to examine them more closely, whereupon the old witch grinned triumphantly.

'Aha!' she cried, closing the lid with a bang and locking it so that the little elf could not escape. 'Take care the red shoes don't pinch your feet, my little bird,' and she set out for her cottage at the other side of the wood.

This time, so determined was she that poor little Jip should not escape, she never once paused, never set down her box, until she was back in her own home.

'Roast elf for supper!' the old witch gloated and she kicked Blackmalkin, who had been working hard all day, patching and darning and sewing and mending, and had just that very moment fallen asleep in front of the fire. 'Go out and bring me fresh wood for the fire so that I can heat the oven, you idle beast,' she cried, and the cat limped out and brought in fresh wood and heaped it on the fire and curled up and went to sleep again.

'Roast elf for supper!' the old witch crooned, and she kicked Blackmalkin a second time. 'Go and draw me fresh water from the well so that I can quench my thirst, you idle beast,' she cried, and the cat plodded wearily out and drew fresh water from the well and poured it into a jug and placed the jug on the table, and then curled up and fell asleep again.

'Roast elf for supper!' the old witch cackled, and she kicked Blackmalkin for the third time. 'Go and bake me a barley loaf to go with my supper, you idle beast,' she cried, and the cat set to work at the kitchen table to bake a barley loaf for his cruel mistress.

'And now, come along, my fine fellow,' the witch cried, opening her pedlar's box and letting out the trembling little Jip. 'Everyone says what a clever fellow you are,' she went on. 'So just open the oven door and tell me if you think it's hot enough for you.' And rubbing her skinny hands together, she started to chuckle at the thought of the treat in store for her.

'Ask her to show you how,' Blackmalkin whispered, brushing past Jip on his way to poke the fire.

'How do I open the oven door?' Jip asked.

'Whoever said that you were clever must have been very much mistaken,' the old witch grumbled. 'Why, like this, of course.' Stretching out her skinny hand, she tugged open the heavy iron door of the oven. 'Now just tell me if it's hot enough for you.'

'Ask her to show you how,' Blackmalkin whispered, brushing past Jip as he returned to the table to bake his barley loaf.

'How do I find out if it's hot enough?' Jip asked.

'A fool!' the old witch cried angrily. 'That's what you are. A complete fool. Why, like this, of course.' Bending nearly double, she put her head and one outstretched arm in the oven.

'Now!' Blackmalkin cried. 'Push with all your might!' And he sprang from the table where he was kneading the barley bread and helped Jip push the witch so that she fell head first into her own oven, and together they slammed shut the heavy door.

'Good riddance to bad rubbish,' Blackmalkin said, piling more and more logs on to the fire so that the flames roared up the wide chimney and licked at the thatch of the roof and then began greedily to devour it. 'Come on!' he cried, and hand in hand he and Jip ran out of the cottage as it began to burn—the cottage and all that was in it.

And Blackmalkin went back with Jip to live in the oak tree which was more than two hundred years old, and everyone— the farmers and their labourers, the village people of Walgrave, Will the Woodman and old Rob the Roadmender and, of course, little Jip and Blackmalkin—rejoiced that there was no longer a wicked witch of Walgrave, and they all lived happily ever after.

2

MOORACHUG AND MEENACHUG

A long, long time ago, when the Little People lived in the land, and all creatures and all things could talk, there dwelt in a hollow hill in the far north of Scotland two quarrelsome creatures called Moorachug and Meenachug.

Moorachug was bad-tempered and Meenachug was lazy, and they were both greedy and very selfish.

One fine October day, Moorachug said to Meenachug,

'Let us take our biggest basket and go out and pick blackberries together, so that you can make me lots of pots of my favourite blackberry jelly.'

'Very well,' said Meenachug, and off they went to the bottom of the hill where the berries were large and shiny and ripe.

And Moorachug picked the berries and dropped them into his basket.

And Meenachug picked the berries—and popped them into her mouth; and whenever Moorachug wasn't looking, she ate his berries too.

All afternoon they worked, but when Moorachug looked at the basket and found it empty, and realized what Meenachug had been doing, then he danced with rage.

'I shall beat you for this!' he screamed, and he rushed off to the nearest willow tree to get a rod to beat Meenachug, because she had eaten all the blackberries he had picked for himself.

'Good afternoon, Moorachug,' said the willow tree. 'What is your news today?'

'All I'm interested in is myself,' Moorachug answered.

'I'm looking for a branch to beat Meenachug with,

because she has eaten all the blackberries I picked for myself.'

'You can't have a branch,' the willow tree replied, 'until you find an axe to cut me.'

And Meenachug went on picking blackberries and popping them into her mouth.

Off Moorachug ran until he came to an axe.

'Good afternoon, Moorachug,' said the axe. 'What news have you today?'

'All I'm interested in is myself,' Moorachug answered.

'I'm looking for an axe to cut the branch to beat Meenachug with,

because she has eaten all the blackberries I picked for myself.'

'You can't have me,' the axe answered, 'until you find a stone to sharpen me.'

And Meenachug went on picking blackberries and popping them into her mouth.

Off Moorachug hurried until he came to a stone.

'Good afternoon, Moorachug,' said the stone. 'What news have you today?'

'All I'm interested in is myself,' Moorachug answered.

'I'm looking for a stone to sharpen the axe,

the axe to cut the branch to beat Meenachug with,

because she has eaten all the blackberries I picked for myself.'

'You can't have me,' the stone replied, 'until you find a river to wet me.'

And Meenachug went on picking blackberries and cramming them into her mouth.

Off Moorachug dashed until he came to a river.

'Good afternoon, Moorachug,' said the river. 'What news have you today?'

'All I'm interested in is myself,' Moorachug answered.

'I'm looking for a river to wet the stone,

the stone to sharpen the axe,

the axe to cut the branch to beat Meenachug with,
because she has eaten all the blackberries I picked for myself.'
'You can't have me,' the river replied, 'until you find a deer to
swim in me.'
And Meenachug went on picking blackberries and cramming
them into her mouth.
On Moorachug hastened until he came to a deer.
'Good afternoon, Moorachug,' said the deer. 'What news have
you today?'
'All I'm interested in is myself,' Moorachug answered.
'I'm looking for a deer to swim in the river,
the river to wet the stone,
the stone to sharpen the axe,
the axe to cut the branch to beat Meenachug with,
because she has eaten all the blackberries I picked for myself.'
'You can't have me,' the deer replied, 'until you find a dog to
chase me.'
And Meenachug went on picking blackberries and cramming
them into her mouth.
On Moorachug raced until he came to a dog.
'Good afternoon, Moorachug,' said the dog. 'What news have
you today?'
'All I'm interested in is myself,' Moorachug answered.
'I'm looking for a dog to chase the deer,
the deer to swim in the river,
the river to wet the stone,
the stone to sharpen the axe,
the axe to cut the branch to beat Meenachug with,
because she has eaten all the blackberries I picked for myself.'
'You can't have me,' the dog replied, 'until you find butter to
rub on my paws.'
And Meenachug went on picking blackberries and cramming
them into her mouth.
On Moorachug sped until he came to a pat of butter.

23

'Good afternoon, Moorachug,' said the butter. 'What news have you today?'

'All I'm interested in is myself,' Moorachug answered.

'I'm looking for butter to rub on the dog's paws,
the dog to chase the deer,
the deer to swim in the river,
the river to wet the stone,
the stone to sharpen the axe,
the axe to cut the branch to beat Meenachug with,
because she has eaten all the blackberries I picked for myself.'

'You can't have me,' the butter replied, 'until you find a mouse to nibble me.'

And Meenachug went on picking blackberries and cramming them into her mouth.

On Moorachug darted until he came to a mouse.

'Good afternoon, Moorachug,' said the mouse. 'What news have you today?'

'All I'm interested in is myself,' Moorachug answered.

'I'm looking for a mouse to nibble the butter,
the butter to rub on the dog's paws;
the dog to chase the deer,
the deer to swim in the river,
the river to wet the stone,
the stone to sharpen the axe,
the axe to cut the branch to beat Meenachug with,
because she has eaten all the blackberries I picked for myself.'

'You can't have me,' the mouse replied, 'until you find a cat to hunt me.'

And Meenachug went on picking blackberries and stuffing them into her mouth.

Off Moorachug scurried until he came to a cat.

'Good afternoon, Moorachug,' said the cat. 'What news have you today?'

'All I'm interested in is myself,' Moorachug answered.

'I'm looking for a cat to hunt the mouse,
the mouse to nibble the butter,
the butter to rub on the dog's paws;
the dog to chase the deer,
the deer to swim in the river,
the river to wet the stone,
the stone to sharpen the axe,
the axe to cut the branch to beat Meenachug with,
because she has eaten all the blackberries I picked for myself.'

'You can't have me,' the cat replied, 'until you find a cow to give me some milk.'

And Meenachug went on picking blackberries and stuffing them into her mouth.

Off Moorachug scrambled until he came to a cow.

'Good afternoon, Moorachug,' said the cow. 'What news have you today?'

'All I'm interested in is myself,' Moorachug answered.

'I'm looking for milk for the cat,
the cat to hunt the mouse,
the mouse to nibble the butter,
the butter to rub on the dog's paws;
the dog to chase the deer,
the deer to swim in the river,
the river to wet the stone,
the stone to sharpen the axe,
the axe to cut the branch to beat Meenachug with,
because she has eaten all the blackberries I picked for myself.'

'You can't have my milk,' the cow replied, 'until you find a cowherd to give me straw.'

And Meenachug went on picking blackberries and shoving them into her mouth.

Off Moorachug scuttled until he came to a cowherd.

'Good afternoon, Moorachug,' said the cowherd. 'What news have you today?'

'All I'm interested in is myself,' Moorachug answered.
'I'm looking for straw for the cow,
the cow to give milk for the cat,
the cat to hunt the mouse,
the mouse to nibble the butter,
the butter to rub on the dog's paws;
the dog to chase the deer,
the deer to swim in the river,
the river to wet the stone,
the stone to sharpen the axe,
the axe to cut the branch to beat Meenachug with,
because she has eaten all the blackberries I picked for myself.'

'You can't have my straw,' the cowherd replied, 'until you get me an oatcake from the farmer's wife.'

And Meenachug went on picking blackberries and shoving them in her mouth.

Off Moorachug bustled until he came to the farmer's wife.

'Good afternoon, Moorachug,' said the farmer's wife. 'What news have you today?'

'All I'm interested in is myself,' Moorachug answered.
'I'm looking for an oatcake for the cowherd,
the cowherd to give straw for the cow,
the cow to give milk for the cat;
the cat to hunt the mouse,
the mouse to nibble the butter,
the butter to rub on the dog's paws;
the dog to chase the deer,
the deer to swim in the river,
the river to wet the stone,
the stone to sharpen the axe,
the axe to cut the branch to beat Meenachug with,
because she has eaten all the blackberries I picked for myself.'

'You can't have an oatcake,' the farmer's wife replied, 'until you bring me some water to mix with the oatmeal.'

'There's nothing to bring water in except that old sieve,' Moorachug said.

'The sieve will do,' the farmer's wife answered.

Away Moorachug limped to the pump, but as fast as he pumped the water into the sieve, as fast it ran through and on to the ground; just as he was going to give up in despair, a hoodie-crow flew overhead and called out,

'Caw, caw, caw. Line it with brown clay and moss. Caw, caw, caw.'

At once Moorachug got to work and lined the sieve with brown clay and moss, and filled it with water from the pump and carried it back to the farmer's wife.

The farmer's wife got to work and baked an oatcake for Moorachug to give to the cowherd,

and the cowherd gave him straw for the cow,

and the cow gave him milk for the cat;

and the cat began to hunt the mouse,

and the mouse began to nibble the butter,

and the butter rubbed itself on the dog's paws;

and the dog began to chase the deer,

and the deer began to swim in the river,

and the river began to wet the stone,

and the stone began to sharpen the axe,

and the axe cut one long branch from the willow tree, so that Moorachug could beat Meenachug because she had eaten all the blackberries he had picked for himself.

But when Moorachug limped back with his rod to the bottom of the hill where, only that morning, the blackberries had grown so large and shiny and ripe, he found that there wasn't one single berry left, and that Meenachug . . .

had . . .

just . . .

BURST!

27

3

THE PRINCESS WHO WANTED TO PLAY
WITH THE STARS

Once upon a time in the not so very long ago, there lived a Little Princess whose parents loved her so dearly that they gave her everything she wanted, just for the pleasure of seeing her smiling and laughing.

Teddy bears, golliwogs, rabbits and ducks; rocking horses, jig-saws, hoops and tops; dolls that walked and dolls that talked —they filled the palace until at last the day came when the Little Princess burst into tears because there was nothing left for her to want.

Day after day she moped and sighed, and the King and Queen sighed to see her so sad, and all the courtiers and royal servants sighed, and everyone throughout the land sighed because there was nothing left for the Little Princess to want.

Everyone, that is, except the Shepherd Boy.

'I have never had a toy in all my life,' he said, when he went home for his supper one evening and his mother told him the news from the palace, 'but each day, while I am watching my sheep, I find something new to amuse me, and each evening, when I look up at the stars in the sky, the sight of them glittering and twinkling makes me happier than if I had all the toys in the world.'

When the Shepherd Boy's mother heard this, she hurried as fast as she could to the palace and told the Guard, and the Guard hurried to the Chamberlain, and the Chamberlain hurried to the King and Queen.

'Your Majesties,' he cried, 'it appears that when the Shepherd Boy looks up at the stars in the sky, the sight of them glittering

and twinkling makes him happier than if he had all the toys in the world.'

'Of course! Why didn't we think of that?' the King and Queen exclaimed, and they hurried to the bedroom of the Little Princess and drew back the curtains so that she could see the stars glittering and twinkling in the sky.

'I want them,' the Little Princess cried, stretching out her hands eagerly. 'I want to play with the stars!' When everyone told her that this was impossible, she burst into tears again and nothing would console her, and long after everyone in the palace had gone to bed, the King and Queen could hear her sobbing,

'I want to play with the stars.'

The next morning the Little Princess woke up very early to find the spring sun shining through the window, and the wood pigeons cooing amongst the white blossom of the pear tree, and immediately she began to think about the stars.

'If no one will give them to me,' she decided, 'then I shall go and find them for myself.'

Putting on her white silken gown, her scarlet shoes and her golden crown, she slipped out of the palace gates while the Guard slept, and whom should she meet but the Shepherd Boy, setting off to watch over his master's sheep.

'Good day to you, Shepherd Boy,' the Little Princess said. 'I am looking for the stars in the sky because I want to play with them. Will you come with me and help me find them?'

'To look at the stars is enough for me,' the Shepherd Boy answered, 'but I will come with you willingly.'

And so the Princess and the Shepherd Boy walked on and they walked on and they walked on, and the Shepherd Boy showed the Little Princess clusters of violets—which he called blue mice—in the hedgerows; and when at length she declared she was tired and wanted to rest, he gathered a handful of yellow cowslips and made them into a tistytosty.

'Never have I seen such a beautiful cowslip ball,' the Little Princess cried, her eyes shining as she held the tistytosty carefully in one hand.

Off they set again, and before long they came to a shallow stream which chuckled and gurgled between its green banks.

'Good day to you, little stream,' the Princess said. 'I am looking for the stars in the sky because I want to play with them. Have you seen them anywhere?'

'Of course I have,' the little stream gurgled. 'They gleam in my water at night. Step in and paddle around and look for yourself.'

The Little Princess took off her red shoes, stepped into the stream, and paddled around and around and around, while the Shepherd Boy sat quietly watching on the bank.

'Not one single star can I see,' the Little Princess cried, and jumping on to the bank, she put on her red shoes, picked up her tistytosty and set off again with the Shepherd Boy.

They walked on and they walked on and they walked on, and the Shepherd Boy showed the Little Princess the tall, purple fritillaries, which he called weeping widows, and when at length she declared she was tired and wanted to rest again, he gathered a handful of yellow-eyed daisies and made her a daisy chain.

'Never have I seen such a beautiful necklace,' the Little Princess cried, her eyes shining as she placed the daisy chain round her neck.

Off they set again and before long they came to an old mill, its wooden wheel creaking and groaning in the deep waters of the mill dam.

'Good day to you, old mill,' the Princess said. 'I am looking for the stars in the sky, because I want to play with them. Have you seen them anywhere?'

'Of course I have,' the old mill rumbled. 'They shine in the waters of the dam at night, twinkling so brightly that I can't get a wink of sleep. Jump in and swim around and look for yourself.'

The Little Princess took off her red shoes, her golden crown and her daisy chain, and jumped into the dam, and swam around and around and around, while the Shepherd Boy sat quietly watching by the mill, holding her tistytosty.

'Not one single star can I see,' the Little Princess cried angrily, and climbing on to the side, she put on her red shoes and golden crown, picked up her tistytosty and her daisy chain, and set off again with the Shepherd Boy.

They walked on and they walked on and they walked on, and the Shepherd Boy showed the Little Princess wild daffodils, which he called lenten lilies, and when at length she declared she was tired and wanted to rest again, he picked a large ox-eye daisy, and pulling off one petal at a time, he told her fortune—

> One for sorrow
> Two for joy,
> Three for a letter,
> Four for a boy,
> Five for silver,
> Six for gold,
> Seven for a secret that's never been told.

'What is the secret that's never been told?' the Little Princess asked, her eyes shining as the last petal fluttered to the ground.

'Wait and see,' the Shepherd Boy answered as they set off again.

Before long they came to a clearing in a dark wood where the Good Folk danced in a ring.

'Good day to you, Good Folk,' the Princess said. 'I am looking for the stars in the sky because I want to play with them. Have you seen them anywhere?'

'Of course we have,' the Good Folk cried. 'They shine on the grass when we dance at night. Join our dance and look for yourself.'

The Little Princess laid down her tistytosty, took off her daisy chain, and joined the ring of the Good Folk, and she danced and

32

danced and danced, while the Shepherd Boy sat quietly watching at the edge of the clearing.

'Oh, dear!' the Little Princess cried at last. 'I've paddled, and I've swum, and I've danced, and not one single star have I seen. Now it looks as though I shall never play with the stars,' and she burst into tears.

At this the Good Folk stopped dancing, shook their heads, and sighed.

'If you'll take our advice you'll turn around and go back to your home,' they said, 'but as we can see that you'll take no advice but your own, then you must walk on and on and on, until at last you come to Four Feet. Ask Four Feet to take you to No Feet At All, and then tell No Feet At All to take you to the Stairs Without Any Steps.'

'And then?' the Little Princess asked.

'If you can climb the Stairs Without Any Steps, you'll be up in the sky, with all the stars to play with.'

'Thank you very much,' the Little Princess cried, and picking up her tistytosty, and putting on her daisy chain, and whispering, 'Seven for a secret that's never been told', she set off again with the Shepherd Boy. They walked on and they walked on and they walked on until at last they came to a horse tied to a weeping willow tree.

'Good day to you, Four Legs,' the Princess cried. 'I'm looking for the stars in the sky because I want to play with them. Have you seen them anywhere?'

'I know nothing of the stars in the sky,' the horse answered. 'I belong to the Good Folk and I do what they tell me.'

'It was the Good Folk who sent us to you,' the Princess answered, 'and they said you were to carry us to No Feet At All.'

'Why didn't you say that in the first place?' the horse grumbled. 'Jump on my back and I'll take you to him.'

The Little Princess and the Shepherd Boy jumped on the back

of Four Feet, and on they rode and on they rode and on they rode, until they came to the edge of the deep, green sea.

'Get down now,' the horse commanded. 'I've brought you to the edge of the sea, and now I must go back.'

'Where is No Feet At All?' the Princess asked, but the horse only shook his mane and galloped back the way he had come.

'There he is,' the Shepherd Boy cried, pointing to a gleaming silver fish which swam through the deep, green sea towards them.

'Good day to you, No Feet At All,' the Princess cried. 'I am looking for the stars in the sky, because I want to play with them. Have you seen them anywhere?'

'I know nothing of the stars in the sky,' the fish answered. 'I belong to the Good Folk and I do what they tell me.'

'It was the Good Folk who sent us to you,' the Princess answered, 'and they said you were to take us to the Stairs Without Any Steps.'

'Why didn't you say that in the first place?' the fish grumbled. 'Jump on my back and I'll take you there.'

The Little Princess and the Shepherd Boy jumped on the back of No Feet At All, and away it swam, on and on and on, until at last they could see ahead a great arc of many coloured lights rising from the sea and curving up to the sky. All the colours of the world it was—red and orange and yellow, green and blue, indigo and violet.

'There you are,' the fish said, when they reached the foot of the rainbow. 'There are the Stairs Without Any Steps, and there are the stars at the other end, glittering and twinkling. Climb up if you can, and play with them as long as you like.'

'To look at the stars is enough for me,' the Shepherd Boy said to the Princess, 'but I will come with you, up the Stairs Without Any Steps.'

Hand in hand they set off, the Princess and the Shepherd Boy; they climbed and they climbed and they climbed, but they never seemed to get any nearer to the glittering, twinkling stars.

34

'It's no good,' the Little Princess cried at last. 'My daisy chain has snapped, and I've lost my tistytosty, and I can't climb the rainbow any more because I am so tired. Now I know that to look at the stars is enough. Please take me back home, Shepherd Boy.'

'You are home, Little Princess.'

And the Princess woke up and found herself safe and sound in bed, with the wood pigeons cooing in the pear tree outside her window.

One for sorrow,

she recited to herself,

Two for joy,
Three for a letter,
Four for a boy,
Five for silver,
Six for gold,
Seven for a secret that's never been told.

She clapped her hands together.

'And the secret that's never been told is finding out for yourself that there are some things you can't have, and being content with all the things you can have.'

'I have decided to give away all my toys to poor children who have none,' she told her parents later that morning.

'All your toys?' the King and Queen said, glad to see the Princess was happy again, and rejoicing because, for the very first time, she was thinking of others.

'All except my teddy bear with only one ear, which I have had since I was a baby.'

'But what will you play with if you give away all your other toys?'

'Could you find me someone who will make me tistytosties

35

and daisy chains, and show me where to find blue mice, and weeping widows, and lenten lilies, and tell my fortune from the petals of the ox-eye daisy?' the Princess asked.

'No one in the kingdom could possibly know all that,' the King and Queen exclaimed.

But there was one person.

Do you know who it was?

Of course.

The Shepherd Boy.

And all that summer, and for many a long summer afterwards, he taught the Little Princess and the other children in the palace all that he knew of flowers and plants, of tistytosties and daisy chains, of blue mice and weeping widows and lenten lilies; and each evening, as the sun sank beneath the western hills, they would look up with shining eyes as one by one the stars came out, the stars which no one—not even a Princess—could play with, but which glittered and twinkled to delight everyone in the whole, wide world.

4

THE WHITE PET

Once upon a time there was a farmer's wife in Scotland who had a pet lamb which followed her around all day and slept in the middle of the kitchen floor at night and was called White Pet.

So well cared for was he that, as the months passed, White Pet grew from being a fine lamb into a very fine sheep; as Christmas approached, the farmer looked at him with approval, rubbed his hands together and smacked his lips.

'White Pet will make us a splendid Christmas dinner,' he said to his wife. 'Remind me to kill him tomorrow.'

'Oho!' said White Pet to himself. 'So my master wants to kill me for Christmas, does he? It's time I was off and away into the wide, wide world to seek my fortune.'

He waited until the farmer and his wife had gone to bed, and then, very quietly, he trotted out of the farmhouse into the cold December night, where the hedges were hung with hoar-frost and the stars glittered in the sky.

On he walked and on he walked until he came to crossroads with a signpost, and by the light of the stars he read 'To the wide, wide world' on one of the arms.

'That is the way for me,' he said, setting off again; but before he had gone very far he met a Bull.

'Hello, Bull,' said White Pet. 'What are you doing out so late on a cold December night?'

'Hello, White Pet,' the Bull answered sadly. 'I'm running away to the wide, wide world to seek my fortune because my master wants to kill me for Christmas.'

'Do you know,' White Pet said, 'that is just what my master

was going to do to me. Why don't you travel with me and we'll seek our fortune together?'

'That's a good idea!' said the Bull, beginning to cheer up; and so White Pet and the Bull set off together, but before they had gone very far they met a Dog.

'Hello, Dog,' said White Pet. 'What are you doing out so late on a cold December night?'

'Hello, White Pet,' the Dog answered mournfully. 'I'm running away to the wide, wide world to seek my fortune because my master thinks I am too old to round up sheep on the mountain side and he has decided to kill me before Christmas.'

'Do you know,' White Pet said, 'that's just what our masters were going to do to us. Why don't you travel with us and we'll seek our fortune together?'

'That's a good idea!' said the Dog, beginning to cheer up straight away; and so White Pet and the Bull and the Dog set off together. But before they had gone very far they met a Cat.

'Hello, Cat,' said White Pet. 'What are you doing out so late on a cold December night?'

'Hello, White Pet,' the Cat answered dejectedly. 'I'm running away to the wide, wide world to seek my fortune because my master thinks I am too old to keep down the mice and rats in the barn, and so he has decided to kill me before Christmas.'

'Do you know,' White Pet said, 'That's just what our masters were going to do to us. Why don't you travel with us and we'll all seek our fortune together?'

'That's a good idea!' said the Cat, cheering up immediately, and so White Pet and the Bull and the Dog and the Cat set off together. But before they had gone very far they met a Cock.

'Hello, Cock,' said White Pet. 'What are you doing out so late on a cold December night?'

'Hello, White Pet,' answered the Cock unhappily. 'I'm running away to the wide, wide world to seek my fortune because my master wants to kill me and eat me for Christmas.'

'Do you know,' White Pet said, 'that's just what our masters were going to do to us. Why don't you travel with us and we'll all seek our fortune together?'

'That's a good idea!' said the Cock, cheering up at once; and so White Pet and the Bull and the Dog and the Cat and the Cock set off together. But before they had gone very far they met a Goose.

'Hello, Goose,' said White Pet. 'What are you doing out so late on a cold December night?'

'Hello, White Pet,' the Goose answered wretchedly. 'I'm running away to the wide, wide world to seek my fortune because my master wants to kill me for his Christmas dinner.'

'Do you know,' White Pet said, 'that's just what our masters were going to do to us. Why don't you travel with us and we'll all seek our fortunes together?'

'That's a good idea!' said the Goose, cheering up at once, and so White Pet and the Bull and the Dog and the Cat and the Cock and the Goose all set off together along the road which led to the wide, wide world.

They had not gone very far in the starlight when they came to a cottage on the edge of a wood; the door of the cottage was closed but from the window streamed a welcoming light.

'Do you think the people here would offer us shelter for the night?' the Bull asked, because he was beginning to feel tired.

'Let us look through the window and find out first what kind of people they are,' White Pet said, and the others nodded their heads and they all crept quietly up to the cottage.

Now the window from which the light was streaming was just the right height for White Pet to see through but the Bull had to lower his head and the Goose had to stretch his neck and the Dog had to stand on his hind legs and the Cat had to jump up on to the window sill and the Cock couldn't see anything, no matter how much he stretched and strained and flapped.

'What's happening inside?' he demanded.

'Sh!' said White Pet. 'In the middle of the room is a table, and in the middle of the table there is a candle burning brightly. Round the table sit six Robbers all busy sharing out a heap of gold and silver coins.'

'This is no place for us,' said the Cat, jumping down from the window sill and preparing to set off again.

'You are mistaken, Cat,' said White Pet. 'It is just the place for us. There is a fire burning on the hearth and a stew cooking in the cauldron over the fire.'

'There are also six Robbers,' said the Dog.

'I have a plan to get rid of them,' said White Pet. 'Now, listen carefully. When I stamp my right foot on the ground I want each one of you to shout as loud as ever you can so that the six of us here will scare the six in there out of their wits. Are you ready? Now!'

White Pet stamped his right foot and suddenly the night was filled with the most fearsome noise of baaing (that was White Pet) and bellowing (that was the Bull) and barking (that was the Dog) and miaowing (that was the Cat) and crowing (that was the Cock) and gobbling (and that, of course, was the Goose).

When they heard the terrible noise, the Robbers turned pale and cried out in alarm and then they scrambled out of their chairs and rushed out of the cottage as fast as they could, pushing and shoving one another out of the way and making for the shelter of the wood as fast as their trembling legs would carry them.

'This cottage will make us a very nice home,' White Pet said, when the Robbers had fled and all was peaceful once more, and the six animals walked in and closed the door to keep out the cold of the December night: they warmed themselves by the Robbers' fire and ate the Robbers' stew and finally they divided up the money which the Robbers had left behind on the table.

'And now we must rest,' said White Pet, yawning loudly because it was long past his bed-time. 'Where will you sleep, Bull?'

'Behind the door as I always have done,' the Bull answerd.

'Where will you sleep, Dog?' White Pet asked.

'Beside the fire, as I always have done,' the Dog answered.

'Where will you sleep, Cat?' White Pet asked.

'In the candle press, as I always have done,' the Cat answered.

'Where will you sleep, Cock?' White Pet asked.

'On the rafters, as I always have done,' the Cock answered.

'And where will you sleep, Goose?' White Pet asked.

'On the midden outside the door, as I always have done,' the Goose answered.

And so they all settled down in the places to which they were accustomed and fell fast asleep, and the candle in the middle of the table burned itself out, and the fire in the hearth died away until only one log flickered faintly.

Meanwhile, in the wood the Robbers shivered and grumbled and talked of the gold and silver they had left behind them in the cottage until finally the Chief Robber cried,

'Wait until the villains are asleep and I will go back and get our money.'

'They must be asleep now,' one of the Robbers said, 'because there is no light shining from the cottage window.'

'Then stay here till I get back,' the Chief Robber said, getting to his feet reluctantly and setting off for the cottage.

Cautiously he pushed open the door, shivering at the strange sounds of heavy breathing which seemed to come from all around him: still shivering, he groped his way in the darkness to the table where they had left their money, but not a coin was on it now.

'The villains have hidden our money,' he thought. 'I must have a light to look for it.'

From the table he groped his way to the candle press, but just as his hand closed on a candle, the Cat clawed him so that he let out a yell of terror. Dashing to the fire, he tried to light the candle from the one flickering log but the Dog woke up, dipped his tail in his bowl of water and shook it over the candle so that it went out. With a terrified shriek the Chief Robber dropped the candle and made for the door, but when he reached the middle of the room White Pet gave him a blow that sent him reeling to the door where the Bull kicked him smartly; in the rafters the Cock crowed and screetched, and as the Chief Robber staggered outside to the midden the Goose belaboured him vigorously with his strong wings.

Shivering and shaking the Chief Robber stumbled back to his gang in the wood.

'I'll never go back to that cottage again. Never!' he moaned. 'You've no idea what I've suffered. The place is haunted by creatures more dreadful than anything I ever imagined. How I live to tell the tale I don't know.

'The place was in darkness and so I went to the candle press to get a candle and a man hiding there stuck ten sharp knives into my hand. (And that, of course, was the Cat.) When I tried to light the candle at the fire a big black man rose up and shook water all over me and the candle. (And that, of course, was the Dog.) I'd had enough then, I can tell you, and all I wanted to do was to get out of the place, but a great hairy man in the middle of the floor attacked me (and that, of course, was White Pet), and a giant behind the door kicked me out (and that, of course, was the Bull), and a little demon up in the roof kept on screaming, "Send him here and I'll do-o-o-o-o for him!" (And that, of course, was the Cock.) Even when I was outside I wasn't safe for a villain on the midden beat me about the legs until they were black and blue. (And that, as you all well know, was the Goose!)

When the robbers heard this and saw how battered and bruised was their Chief, they decided that the sooner they were away from that part of Scotland, the better it would be, and they set off running there and then and for all I know, they're running still.

As for White Pet and his five companions, they decided that they weren't particularly interested in seeing the wide, wide world, after all, and that what they really wanted was a good home, enough to eat and pleasant company and so, with the money that the Robbers had left behind, they settled down in the cottage and lived there happily and contentedly for many a long year.

5

CHILDE ROWLAND AND
THE KING OF ELFLAND

In the days when elves and fairies lived in secret places throughout
the fair land of Scotland, and brought sorrow and trouble to those
who, however unwittingly, offended them or broke their laws,
there dwelt in the Borderland, not far from the River Tweed, a
Queen with four children—three sons, of whom the youngest was
called Childe* Rowland, and one fair daughter named Burd†
Helen.

Now it happened that one Midsummer's Eve as the three
brothers were playing with a ball in the meadow beside the
church, the eldest brother kicked the ball so hard and so high that
it soared over the steeple of the church and disappeared among the
trees on the opposite side.

'Burd Helen,' the eldest brother called out to his sister. 'Go and
find the ball which I have kicked so high and which has fallen
among the trees on the far side of the church,' and Burd Helen,
who loved her three brothers dearly and delighted in doing things
to please them, picked up the long skirts of her silken gown and
ran off withershins (counter-clockwise) round the church, in
search of the missing ball, while her brothers, tired out by their
play, lay down in the meadow and chewed the long, succulent
stems of the grass flowers and talked of this and of that.

When twilight fell and Burd Helen had not returned with the
ball, the three brothers set off in search of her, walking round the
church in the opposite direction from that taken by their sister,

* Childe n. (A.S. cild): a youth of gentle birth.
† Burd n. (obs.: ety. obscure): a maiden, a lady.

45

but there was no sign of her there, or amongst the trees on the far side, and so they hurried home to the Queen, their mother.

'Lady Mother,' said the eldest son, 'we were playing with a ball and I kicked it so hard and so high that it soared over the steeple of the church, and Burd Helen went to look for it and now she has disappeared.'

'Which way did she go round the church?' the Queen asked.

'Withershins,' the eldest son answered.

'Withershins on Midsummer's Eve!' the Queen cried in alarm. 'She should have gone as the sun journeys, from east to west, and not withershins. Now she has delivered herself into the power of the King of Elfland and only Merlin the Magician can tell where she has been hidden.'

'Do not fear, Lady Mother,' said the eldest son. 'I will go to Merlin and find out from him where the King of Elfland has hidden our sister and I will bring her back to you.'

With his mother and his younger brother and Childe Rowland to help him, he put on his shining armour and his helmet with the golden plume, and buckling his sword to his side, he set off on his Barbary roan: over the green hills he rode and through the pleasant valleys, fording the broad River Tweed and many a smaller stream besides, until at length he reached the yellow sand and the grey sea and the mighty castle of Joyous Garde in Northumbria, where the magician was staying with King Arthur's gallant knight, the famous Sir Launcelot.

When the eldest son explained why he had come, the servants led him to the library where Merlin read among ancient books, handwritten on sheepskin, and gravely the magician listened as the eldest son told him how he had kicked the ball high over the church and how Burd Helen had disappeared when she went to look for it.

'Which way did she go round the church?' Merlin asked.

'Withershins,' the eldest brother answered.

'Withershins on Midsummer's Eve,' Merlin said thoughtfully. 'On any other evening it would have made no difference, but on Midsummer's Eve she should have gone as the sun journeys, from east to west, and not withershins. She has delivered herself into the power of the King of Elfland, and only the boldest knight in the whole of Christendom can rescue her.'

'Tell me what to do to save her,' the eldest brother said, but so eager was he to be off that he only half listened to what Merlin had to say, and then, with a hasty word of thanks, he spurred his horse back to the River Tweed and the green rolling hills of the Scottish Lowlands.

The days passed. And the weeks. And when the eldest brother did not return to his home or send any word, his lady mother, the Queen, knew that by some mischance he must have delivered himself into the power of the King of Elfland.

'Do not fear, Lady Mother,' said the second son. 'I will go to Merlin and find out from him where the King of Elfland has hidden our sister and our brother and I will bring them back to you.'

With his mother and Childe Rowland to help him, he put on his shining armour and his helmet with the silver plume, and buckling his sword to his side, he set off on his jet black stallion for Joyous Garde on the coast of Northumbria.

So eager was he to find his brother and his sister that he only half listened to what Merlin the Magician had to say, and then, with a hasty word of thanks, he left the castle and spurred his horse back to the River Tweed and the green rolling hills of the Scottish Lowlands.

Again the days passed. And the weeks. And when the second brother did not return to his home or send any word, his lady mother, the Queen, knew that by some mischance he must have delivered himself into the power of the King of Elfland.

'Do not worry, sweet Lady Mother,' Childe Rowland said. 'I will go to Merlin and find out from him where the King of Elf-

47

land has hidden my sister and my two elder brothers, and with his help I will bring them safely back to you.'

But Childe Rowland, because he was the youngest son, had no shining suit of armour to put on, no helmet with waving plume, and he would have had no sword had not the Queen lifted down from the wall of the castle his father's sword of finest Toledo steel; and so it was, in his shabby doublet and faded hose, mounted on an old grey nag which ambled along at a speed which he might have equalled had he been on foot, that Childe Rowland eventually came to Joyous Garde and begged Merlin to help him.

'The King of Elfland has stolen away Burd Helen and tricked your brothers so that they are in his power,' Merlin said, 'and only the boldest knight in the whole of Christendom can rescue them.'

'Tell me what I must do and I shall try to do it,' Childe Rowland said, and he sat down on a stool and listened carefully.

'Ride with all speed back to your own country,' Merlin said, 'and at the moment when the last ray of the setting sun disappears below the horizon, you will see before you a grassy hill, and in front of the hill a rowan tree hung with bright red berries. Dismount and tie your horse to the rowan tree; walk three times withershins round the hill and then call out, "Open, door!" and a door in the hillside will open and you will find yourself in the Dark Tower of Elfland.

'Remember that from the moment you pass the rowan tree, you will be in Fairyland and the King will use all his powers to trap you as he has trapped your brothers. It behoves you, therefore, to remember two things: should anyone speak to you, give no answer, but cut off his head with your father's sword, and whatever befalls, bite no bite and drink no drink or you will never see the fair land of Scotland again.'

Childe Rowland thanked Merlin, and was just about to go when the magician motioned him to wait.

'When you meet the King of Elfland,' he said, 'his sword will be a magic one, but I shall match him spell for spell. Give me your father's sword and I shall work a charm which will make it invincible in your hands.'

Again Childe Rowland thanked Merlin, and with his invincible sword by his side, he went out to where he had left his old grey nag. To his surprise, the horse had grown young and lively in his absence, and as soon as he mounted it, it set off at a gallop for the River Tweed and the green rolling hills of the Scottish Lowlands, and just as the last ray of the setting sun disappeared below the horizon, Childe Rowland saw before him a grassy hill, and in front of the hill a rowan tree hung with bright red berries.

Dismounting, he tied his horse to the tree and set off to walk withershins round the hill but he had not circled it once before a swineherd suddenly appeared beside him.

'You look tired, stranger,' the swineherd said. 'Will you not enter my cottage and rest awhile?'

Remembering what Merlin had said, Childe Rowland made no answer, but drawing his father's sword he cut off the swineherd's head, whereupon the elfin creature disappeared with a shriek of rage.

He had not circled the hill twice before a cowherd suddenly appeared before him.

'You look weary, stranger,' the cowherd said. 'Will you not enter my cottage and rest awhile?'

Remembering what Merlin had said, Childe Rowland made no answer, but drawing his father's sword a second time, he cut off the cowherd's head, whereupon the creature disappeared with a scream of rage.

He had not circled the hill three times before a henwife suddenly appeared in front of him.

'You look exhausted, stranger,' the henwife said. 'Will you not enter my cottage and rest awhile?'

Childe Rowland was now so tired that he would have accepted her invitation gladly, but just in time he remembered Merlin's warning, and drawing his father's sword, he cut off the henwife's head, whereupon she too disappeared with a baffled shriek.

'Open, door!' he cried, when at last he had circled the hill three times withershins, and immediately a door in the hillside opened, and Childe Rowland bent his head and entered, and found himself in the Dark Tower of Elfland.

Here there was neither sun nor moon, nor was there a single star, but the place was lit fitfully by the unearthly gleam of precious stones which studded the walls, so that now the Dark Tower was green with the radiance of emeralds, now blue with the light of sapphires, now yellow with the glitter of topazes, now white with the cold, chill gleam of diamonds.

When Childe Rowland's eyes became accustomed to the strange, ever-changing light, he saw that he was in a great hall, and at the far end, on a crystal throne, sat his sister, Burd Helen, while on crystal couches on either side of her lay his brothers, their eyes closed as they slept a sleep as deep as death.

Eagerly Childe Rowland embraced his sister and long did they talk, while around them the light gleamed fitfully green and blue and amber and white as the emeralds and sapphires, topazes and diamonds glittered on the dark walls; and Burd Helen told her brother how the King of Elfland had stolen her away because she had run withershins round the church on Midsummer's Eve, and how he had bewitched her so that she could not leave the Dark Tower until the spell was broken: and she told him how her two brothers had come to rescue her but had been tricked by the King, so that now they lay on their crystal couches, their eyes closed as they slept a sleep as deep as death.

Long, long they talked together until Childe Rowland, who had ridden far and hard that day, began to feel weak and faint from exhaustion.

'Will you not offer me meat to stay my hunger and drink to quench my thirst?' he asked his sister.

Sorrowfully she looked at him, but the Elf King's spell pre-

vented her saying anything to warn him, and she brought him a silver goblet filled to the brim with a clear liquid.

Eagerly Childe Rowland took the silver goblet and raised it to his lips, but just as he was about to take the first sip he remembered Merlin's warning to bite no bite and drink no drink if he wished to see again the fair land of Scotland, and he dashed the goblet to the ground where the liquid hissed and spluttered and bubbled and boiled and finally disappeared in a choking, yellow smoke.

At that moment a terrible cry rang out through the hall and the Elf King strode in, his face dark with anger, and the green and the blue and the yellow and the white lights of the precious stones were reflected from the blade of the magic sword which he carried in his right hand.

'What human dares set foot in the Dark Tower of Elfland?' he cried, and his voice echoed and re-echoed among the rafters in the darkness of the ceiling.

'My name is Childe Rowland and I am come for my sister and my two brothers,' Childe Rowland answered, and drawing his father's sword he advanced to where the Elf King awaited him, and the great hall rang with the clash of steel on steel, but the spell which Merlin had wrought was more powerful than any magic of the Elf King's, and the Toledo blade was indeed invincible in the hands of Childe Rowland, so that ere long the King fell on his knees and begged for mercy.

'Take the spell from Burd Helen and restore my brothers to life,' Childe Rowland commanded, returning his father's sword to its scabbard.

Without a word the defeated king went out of the hall and when he returned he was carrying a flask of red liquid which smelled of freshly mown grass and newly gathered violets and ripe apples ready to drop at the touch of a hand.

Dipping his long fingers into the flask, the Elf King sprinkled the red liquid on the two sleeping brothers, making sure that it touched their closed eyelids and their ears, their nostrils and their lips, their toes and their finger tips. As the brothers sighed and stirred and slept, and sighed and stirred again, he turned to Burd Helen on her crystal throne and spoke to her in his own language in a voice so soft and sad that two tears formed in her eyes and fell to the ground where they turned into pearls.

'Now you are free,' the Elf King said, and he picked up the two pearls which had been tears and placed them in a golden box, and he sighed because he had lost Burd Helen, whom he had hoped to make his bride.

But Burd Helen had already forgotten all about him as she kissed and embraced her brothers, and, laughing and rejoicing, they left the hall and went out into the starry night. And Childe Rowland set Burd Helen on his horse and the three brothers walked beside her and when they neared their home they saw the light streaming from all the windows of the castle where the Queen, their mother, awaited them, and in the church tower the bells pealed joyfully to welcome back Childe Rowland who had rescued Burd Helen and his brothers from the Dark Tower of the King of Elfland.

6

PEREGRINE AND THE REDMAN
OF ROCKINGHAM FOREST

Many hundreds of years ago, when the royal Forest of Rockingham stretched from Northampton on the River Nene north to Stamford on the Welland, and the country people of Northamptonshire were hard put to it to find a way to earn an honest living, there dwelt an old man who had three sons named John and Mark and Peregrine.

John, the eldest, was a burly giant of a fellow who could fell a tree in half the time it took anyone else, but he spoke little and thought even less.

Mark, the second son, was small and slight, useless where strength was needed, but clever when it came to thinking out a problem and cunning when he wished to persuade others to do what he wanted.

As for Peregrine, the youngest son, he cared neither for hard work nor for sitting thinking: he would lend a willing ear to anyone's troubles, give a helping hand to anyone in distress, and, when he was alone, nothing pleased him more than to whistle and sing as he fashioned strange creatures from bits of wood which he found in the forest.

The old man, feeling that his days were drawing to a close, called his three sons to his bedside, sighed heavily, and turned first to his eldest son, John.

'All my life I have been poor,' he said, 'and what little money I have made has been spent feeding and clothing the four of us. All that I have to leave you is a cauldron to cook your dinner in, a tripod to hang it on, and three wooden stools to sit on. Share them with your three brothers and remember that you are the strongest and must look after the other two."

He then turned to his second son, Mark.

'All that I have to leave you,' he said, 'is my longbow made from the good yew tree, my arrows feathered from the grey goose's wing, my axe and my hunting knife. Share them with your brothers and remember that you are the cleverest and must look after the other two.'

When he turned to Peregrine, his youngest son, he sighed again.

'All that I possess I have given to your brothers because I know full well that if a beggar asked you for the shirt off your back, you would give it to him and go cold yourself. I might offer you words of advice except that I know that what goes in one of your ears flies out of the other. Your brothers will look after you and share what they have with you, but remember that should the time come, you in your turn must share what you possess with them.'

A few weeks later the old man died, whereupon the farmer who owned the cottage told the three sons that as there was no work for them on his land, he could not have them living there, and he ordered them to leave the cottage within twenty-four hours or he would have them thrown out.

Sadly the brothers packed up their meagre possessions. John, the burly giant, carried the cauldron and the tripod and the three wooden stools and strode off, not knowing what was to become of them because he was not very good at thinking.

Mark, who was clever when it came to working out a problem, carried the longbow and the arrows, the axe and the hunting knife and followed John, thinking hard of where they might find a new home.

As for Peregrine, he carried a jar of preserved ginger given him by the daughter of the master woodcarver of Wellingborough Church and he followed his brothers, whistling cheerfully because the May dew was glittering on the green grass and the birds were singing so sweetly in the quickening hedgerows.

On and on the three brothers walked until at last they came to the outskirts of the royal Forest of Rockingham, and there John, the eldest, would have turned aside, because he knew that the Forest belonged to the King of England and was patrolled by his keepers so that no one could cut down trees for fuel or shoot the deer for food.

'Don't stop,' Mark said. 'Go on.'

'But what if the King's keepers find us?' John asked.

'The Forest is big enough for them and for us,' Mark answered.

And so they made their way deeper and deeper into the Forest of Rockingham, avoiding the paths and the rides and forcing a way through shrubs and hollies and ferns until, just as the sun was setting they came to a little clearing by a stream, where there stood an old cottage with a thatched roof, which sagged and slipped to reveal the wooden timbers underneath.

'Stop here,' said Mark, putting down the longbow and the arrows, the axe and the hunting knife, and he prowled around looking for signs of human beings in the clearing, but there were none.

'No one has lived in this cottage for many a long year,' he said. 'We shall be safe enough here.'

'But there is hardly any roof and the door is falling off its hinges,' John said after staring at the old cottage for a long time, still carrying the cauldron and the tripod and the three wooden stools.

'And the mice and spiders and rabbits have made it their home,' Peregrine added, peering through the dirty window.

'The roof can be re-thatched,' Mark answered, 'and the door re-hung, and as for the mice and spiders and rabbits, why they must find themselves new homes.'

That night the three brothers slept in the open air, in the little clearing by the stream, and the next morning Mark cut some branches from an elder bush and fashioned a broom from them and gave this to John to sweep out the cottage and he sent Peregrine to cut reeds from the stream so that he could re-thatch the cottage roof, but Peregrine was so fascinated by the shoals of minnows darting about in the sunlight that he forgot all about the reeds and Mark, very annoyed, had to come and do the work himself.

As the days passed, the cottage became clean and neat: the roof was re-thatched, the door re-hung and Mark built a ladder to lead to a little room under the eaves where they could store their food and possessions.

Once they had a comfortable home, Mark set about organising their days, so that one of the brothers would stay near the cottage and collect fresh bracken for them to sleep on at night and cut wood for the fire and prepare and cook the evening meal, while the other two brothers would roam the Forest of Rockingham in search of food, snaring rabbits and hares and badgers, bringing down partridges and plovers and pheasants and occasionally shooting a fine red deer.

Mark planned. And John worked. And Peregrine? He whistled and sang and thought how good it was to be alive, and when he was sent hunting for food, he would pause beside the brook and lose himself in daydreams and return home with a handful of scarlet pimpernels, which he called Poor Man's Weather-glass because the flowers closed the moment the sun went in: and when he was left at home to prepare the food for the hungry hunters, he would sit outside and lose himself in the delight of fashioning strange creatures from pieces of wood—rabbits and hares and badgers, partridges and plovers and pheasants and fine red deer and there would be nothing for his brothers to eat when they returned home, hungry from their hunting.

Now one day, when the leaves on the oak were turning yellow and the beech was red-gold in the sunlight, it was John's turn to stay at home and prepare the meal.

First he chopped up part of an old beech tree which he had cut down several weeks previously, and carrying the wood into the cottage he lit a fine fire in the big, open fireplace and over this he placed the iron tripod he had brought from his father's cottage. Then he went down to the stream, half filled the cauldron with clear water, hung it on the tripod over the fire and dropped into it large pieces of juicy meat from the deer which Mark had tracked down and shot with his father's longbow and one of the arrows feathered from the grey goose's wing.

Soon the cottage began to fill with the delicious smell of gently cooking venison and John smacked his lips in anticipation of the meal they would have that evening and then sat down in front of the fire to fashion himself a new pair of boots from the hide of the deer.

So engrossed was he in his work that he did not notice the little Redman who peered slyly in at the open door of the cottage, sniffed appreciatively, and then advanced to the fire where the venison was bubbling in the iron cauldron.

'Please will you give me a little broth?' the little creature said, holding out a wooden bowl.

John looked up from the boot he was making and for several seconds he stared at the hairy little man in the shabby red clothes, with the red cap on his untidy hair, and all the time he kept turning over and over in his mind what the little Redman had asked.

'Give you some of my stew?' he said at last. 'Why should I do that? My father said that I had to look after my two brothers but he didn't say anything about looking after a little Redman. If you want venison stew, go and shoot a deer for yourself. Now go away!'

The little Redman went to the door, waited until John was engrossed in his work once more, and then creeping softly back, he dipped his wooden bowl in the cauldron.

'Put that back!' John cried, lumbering to his feet, but the little

Redman with a triumphant laugh bounded across the clearing to a track which led through the forest.

With a cry of anger John picked up his axe and ran after him, never noticing the trailing briar which the little Redman had left across the track, so that just as John reached out his hand to grab the little creature, the briar caught him round the ankle and he crashed to the ground, the axe flying out of his hand and landing in a dense clump of nettles. By the time he had struggled to his feet and found his axe the little Redman with his bowl of venison broth was nowhere to be seen, and there was nothing for John to do but hunt for a dock leaf to rub on his hand where the nettles had stung it.

When his brothers returned that evening and heard how the little Redman had helped himself to their venison stew, Peregrine laughed, but Mark was very angry.

'We have barely enough food for ourselves,' Mark said, 'and we're certainly not going to start feeding the Little People as well.'

'Surely we can spare enough for one,' Peregrine pleaded.

'It won't stop at one,' Mark answered. 'The next day there'll be two, and the day after that the whole family will come, and before we know what's what we'll be feeding all the Little People in Rockingham Forest. Tomorrow I'll stay at home and deal with the little Redman.' And he passed his bowl back to John for a second helping of the delicious stew.

The next day John and Peregrine set out hunting and Mark stayed behind. After he had chopped the wood and lit the fire and hung the cauldron on the tripod over it, he dropped in large pieces of juicy meat from the deer he had shot with his father's longbow and one of the arrows feathered from the grey goose's wing.

Soon the cottage began to fill with the delicious smell of gently cooking venison. Mark smacked his lips in anticipation of the meal they would have that evening and then sat down in front of the fire to fashion himself new arrows, each one yard in length, from the pliant wood of the ash and the birch.

So engrossed was he in his work that he did not notice the little Redman who peered slyly in at the open door of the cottage, sniffed appreciatively, and then advanced to the fire where the venison was bubbling in the iron cauldron.

'Please will you give me a little broth?' the little creature said, holding out his wooden bowl.

'My father said that I had to look after my two brothers but he didn't say anything about looking after a little Redman,' Mark answered, and putting down the arrow he was making, he gave the little creature a long lecture on how difficult life was and how everyone must work for himself and find his own food.

The little man appeared to be listening attentively, and Mark got so carried away by the sound of his own voice, that he did not notice the little creature sidle up to the cauldron and dip his wooden bowl in it.

'Put that back!' he cried, leaping to his feet, but the little Redman, with a triumphant laugh, bounded across the clearing to the track which led through the forest. With a cry of anger Mark snatched up his knife and ran after him, never noticing the trailing ivy which the little Redman had left across the track, so that just as Mark reached out his hand to grab the little creature, the ivy caught him round the ankle and he crashed to the ground, his knife flying out of his hand and landing in a dense clump of spear thistles. By the time he had struggled to his feet and found his knife, the little Redman with his bowl of venison broth was nowhere to be seen, and there was nothing for Mark to do but to pick the sharp spines of the thistles out of his hand.

When the other two brothers returned that evening and heard how the little Redman had outwitted the clever Mark and helped himself once more to their venison stew, Peregrine laughed, but John was very angry.

'Seeing you think it's such a joke,' Mark said, 'let's see how you deal with the little Redman tomorrow.'

So it was that the following day the two older brothers, John and Mark, set out hunting and Peregrine stayed behind. He chopped the wood, lit the fire and prepared the venison stew in the iron cauldron: when it began to simmer he added a pinch of salt, a pinch of pepper, a branch of fennel and some wild thyme, and as soon as the cottage began to fill with the delicious smell of gently cooking venison, he sat down with a branch of oakwood and began to fashion it into the figure of a mermaid with flowing hair and the tail of a fish.

So engrossed was he in his carving that he did not notice the little Redman who peered slyly in at the open door, sniffed appreciatively, and then advanced to the fire where the venison bubbled in the iron cauldron.

'Please will you give me a little broth?' the little creature said, holding out his wooden bowl.

'Help yourself,' Peregrine answered, gesturing with his knife towards the pot, and as the little Redman did so, he stood up, walked to the door, closed it, and then leaning against it, continued carving his oak mermaid.

'You look hungry,' Peregrine said. 'Sit down beside the fire and eat the stew.'

Looking rather surprised, the little man sat down and gulped the stew noisily and with obvious pleasure.

'Have some more,' Peregrine suggested.

The little Redman filled his bowl a second time and again he gulped down the contents noisily.

'Now I must go,' he said, advancing to the door against which Peregrine leaned, carving his oak mermaid.

Looking down, Peregrine shook his head and said never a word.

'Let me out!' the little man commanded, stamping his right foot and turning into a prickly hedgehog.

'Just the thing for tomorrow's meal,' Peregrine exclaimed. 'If there's one dish I like above all others it's baked hedgehog flavoured with sage.'

'Let me out!' the hedgehog cried, stamping its right foot and turning into a bee and flying round the room in search of some way of escape.

'Just the creature to bring me some honey,' Peregrine cried. 'If there's one drink I've wanted since we came to Rockingham Forest it's been a beaker of mead made from the best honey.'

'Let me out!' the bee cried, stamping its right hind foot and turning into a snake.

'Just the thing to make me a new belt,' Peregrine cried. 'If there's one thing I've wanted since we came to Rockingham Forest it's a snakeskin belt.'

'What will you take to let me out of here?' the snake asked, changing back into a little Redman again.

'What can you offer?' Peregrine asked.

'All the gold you can carry,' the Redman replied.

'Done!' said Peregrine, and opening the door he followed the little creature across the clearing and along a winding path in the deep, tangled forest and down the steep side of a valley to an old stone well.

Down the well climbed the little Redman, and after him climbed Peregrine, and when they reached the bottom, instead of there being water, there was a passage which led to a cave, and the floor of the cave was covered with shining, gleaming, glittering golden coins.

'Help yourself,' the little Redman said.

'Thank you,' Peregrine answered, and he filled the pockets of his coat and his breeches with golden coins which shone and gleamed and glittered.

'One good turn deserves another,' he said to the little creature. 'Every year, when the hunter's moon rides full in the sky, I will come here and bring you a large bowl of venison stew.'

Climbing out of the well, Peregrine made his way back to the cottage, and there he emptied the gold from his coat pockets and piled it in front of the kitchen fire for his brothers to find and to do with as they thought fit.

'All these years they have looked after me,' he thought, 'and now at last I can help to look after them.'

With the gold in the pocket of his breeches and his knife in one hand and the oak mermaid in the other he set off through the Forest of Rockingham, whistling and singing until he came to the stone town of Wellingborough, which slumbered where the River Ise joins the River Nene, and as he passed the workshop by the church with the soaring spire he saw the woodcarver at his bench carving roses to decorate the seats in the choir.

'Could you do with an apprentice to help you?' Peregrine asked, showing the old man the mermaid which he had carved.

'Perhaps,' the old craftsman said cautiously, 'but first let me see what you can do with that.'

He gave Peregrine a fine block of wood and Peregrine sat down and started to carve, and under his hand the wood became the old master woodcarver working at his bench and carving roses. The old man was so pleased with Peregrine's work that he accepted him as an apprentice immediately and took him home to live with him, and together they worked on the carvings for the church with the soaring spire.

When Peregrine had served his apprenticeship, he bought a big stone house in Wellingborough with the golden coins given him by the little Redman, and he married the master woodcarver's daughter who, you may remember, had given him a jar of preserved ginger to take with him on that May day when he had first set out with his brothers to find a new home.

And they prospered—Peregrine and his wife and their many children, but every year, when the hunter's moon rode full in the sky, Peregrine would set off for the well in Rockingham Forest, carrying a wooden bowl of venison stew for the little Redman.

And should you ever be passing through Wellingborough, which lies where the River Ise joins the River Nene, and should you have time to visit the stone church with the soaring spire which stands there to this day, go into the chancel and lift up the

wooden seats in the choir, and underneath you will see the mermaid, and the old master craftsman carving roses, and a lion and
an eagle and a fox and a goose—all carved by Peregrine so many
hundreds of years ago.

7

THE LAIDLEY WORM
OF SPINDLESTONE HEUGH

Once upon a time there dwelt a widowed king in the great castle of Bamburgh, which even today crowns the top of a mighty rock and overlooks the grey North Sea and the distant Farne Islands.

This king had one daughter, the Lady Margaret, who was as good and kind as she was beautiful, and one son, Childe Wynd, who was gallant and handsome and brave. Because there was nothing to occupy him in Northumbria, Childe Wynd had sailed across the grey North Sea with three and thirty men in search of adventure, but the Lady Margaret stayed at home to look after her widowed father.

All the courtiers and all the servants, down to the smallest scullery maid and the youngest page, loved the Lady Margaret because she was so good and kind, and when she rode on her milk-white pony through the village and into the countryside, the men stopped working in the fields and the women and children hurried to their doors and windows to wave to her and to see her smile and hear her joyful laughter.

'What should I do without my precious Margaret?' the king would say, stroking her flaxen hair as she sat beside him on a silken cushion, reading to him of the life of St Cuthbert who once had lived on the distant Farne Islands.

'What should I do without my precious Margaret?' the king would say, as he sat down to the meals which she had ordered and very often had helped to prepare with her own hands.

'What should I do without my precious Margaret?' he would say, watching her as she went about her household tasks, laughing with happiness as she saw that all was ordered as a great castle should be.

But alas! the day came when the king forgot the Lady Margaret with her blue eyes and flaxen hair and dancing smile. He had journeyed to the court of a neighbouring king to settle a dispute about boundaries, and here he met a princess with hair as dark as the wood of the blackthorn in early spring, and skin as white as its blossom, and eyes that were cold and strange and green, and nothing would content him but that the princess should marry him there and then.

'How happy I am for my father, the king,' the Lady Margaret said, when messengers brought her the news of the king's marriage, and she gave orders for a great feast to be prepared and a ball to be held in honour of the new queen on the evening of her arrival at Bamburgh.

When the king journeyed back through the fair land of Northumbria and heard all his people praising the beauty of their new queen, he rejoiced, and when he rode up the winding path to his castle on the top of the rock and the Lady Margaret stepped forward to welcome him and to hand to the new queen the keys of the household, he thought himself the happiest of men to have so fair a daughter and so beautiful a wife.

But the courtiers at the ball that evening eyed the new queen doubtfully, for they were wise in the ways of the world and they recognised that she was not as other princesses were.

'She has bewitched the king,' they whispered amongst themselves. 'We must beware of her because she has evil powers.' And because they feared her, they praised her to her face, telling her that she was the most beautiful woman in the whole of fair Northumbria, and she was well pleased, and smiled with her mouth but not with her cold green eyes.

But amongst the courtiers there was one old Border chieftain whose home was on the slopes of Cheviot itself: he was honest and forthright and always spoke the truth, and he loved the Lady

Margaret because she reminded him of his own daughter who had died many years before. Now he turned to the courtiers and gazed at them scornfully.

'Often have I heard you say that the Lady Margaret, who is as good as she is kind, was the most beautiful in all of fair Northumbria: tonight I see no reason why any of you should change your minds!'

When the new queen heard this her face darkened and her green eyes flashed.

'There is not room for the Lady Margaret and me in this fair kingdom of Northumbria,' she thought. 'The Lady Margaret must go.' The courtiers had been right: the new queen did indeed possess evil powers—because she was a witch.

The next day, pleading that she was tired and must rest after the long journey and the festivities, the witch-queen climbed the spiral staircase to the topmost room of the main tower which overlooked the grey North Sea, and there she read deeply in her books of magic, and finally she brewed a spell of great power and, smiling with triumph, returned to her own room and fell into a deep sleep.

Great was the consternation in the royal castle the next morning when it was discovered that the Lady Margaret was nowhere to be found. Distraught, the king ordered the castle to be searched from attic to cellars, and although the sentries on duty swore that she had not left the castle during the night, messengers were sent throughout the surrounding countryside to enquire if anyone had seen the king's fair daughter. But all was in vain. The Lady Margaret had vanished completely.

'The new queen knows something about this,' the courtiers muttered among themselves, but because they were afraid of her they were careful not to let her hear what they were saying.

'Now I am the most beautiful in the whole of fair Northumbria,' the witch-queen said, and she brewed a powerful drink and with her own white hands she gave it to the king and the courtiers so that they would forget the Lady Margaret altogether. But the old chieftain who loved the Lady Margaret as his own daughter, had returned to his home on the slopes of Cheviot, and he did not drink of the witch-queen's brew and he alone mourned for the king's fair daughter.

And then one day, as the king and his courtiers sat in the great hall of the castle, listening to a minstrel singing a sad song of a Border battle fought long before, a terrified countryman pushed his way past the guards and the listening courtiers and flung himself on one knee in front of the king.

'Help us, good king,' he cried. 'A laidley worm has made its home in the cave in Spindlestone Heugh. Every day it demands from us the milk of seven cows, and every day it grows bigger and bigger: so poisonous is its breath that nothing will grow for seven long miles in every direction.'

'A loathsome dragon?' the king said. 'But what help can I give you?'

'Send someone to kill the laidley worm,' the countryman begged, 'for though it has done us no harm, it is so big and terrifying that it frightens the stoutest man amongst us.'

The king looked round the hall at his courtiers and soldiers and his brow grew sad, because the witch-queen had cast her spell on them so that they were all afraid and none dare offer to kill the loathsome dragon. Only the old chieftain from the Borders had no fear of the witch-queen, and now he stepped forward and stood in front of the king.

'When I was a young man,' he cried, 'my eye was as keen as a hawk's, my ear could hear the feet of the wind as it ruffled the heather moors and my right arm was stronger than that of any man in the whole of Northumbria. Many a laidley worm and fearsome sea monster have I slain when I was young, but now I am old and unfit for such deeds of valour. Now there is but one hero to whom such a task could be entrusted.

'Make me your messenger, sire,' said the old chieftain, 'and let me voyage across the grey North Sea in search of your son, Childe Wynd, and bring him back to rid your kingdom of this loathsome dragon.'

Immediately the sadness left the king's face.

'Go with all speed,' he cried, 'and bid my son, Childe Wynd, return to help us here in our great need.'

As soon as she heard this, the witch-queen left the hall, climbed the spiral staircase to the topmost room of the main tower which overlooked the grey North Sea, and opened her books of magic again.

'When it is time for the loathsome dragon to die, I shall kill it with my spells,' she said to herself. 'But because Childe Wynd is noble and brave and has always loved his sister, the Lady Margaret, he must not be allowed to return to Northumbria, lest he finds out what I have done.'

And once again she brewed a spell of great power, and each day after that she sat at the window of the topmost room of the main tower, staring out over the cold grey sea, until at last she spied the sails of Childe Wynd's ship on the horizon.

With a triumphant laugh she conjured up a terrible storm, so that huge waves dashed against the sides of the ship and broke on the deck and howling winds tore the sails to ribbons: three times Childe Wynd tried to beach his ship on the yellow sands of Northumbria and three times the witch-queen drove him back with her spells.

'What can I do now?' Childe Wynd cried. 'This is no ordinary storm which three times has forced us back from land.'

'You are right,' said the old Border chieftain. 'This storm is the work of a witch—but I shall name no names until you name her for yourself. And now you must listen to me and accept my advice, for though I am no longer the mighty warrior I once was, my years have brought me great knowledge and cunning. We must return, you and I and your three and thirty men at arms to your home over the sea, and there you must build yourself a new ship and shape your masts from the rowan tree and make your sails from the finest silk.'

Childe Wynd did as the old chieftain advised, returning to his home across the sea, where he built a new ship and shaped the masts from the rowan tree and made the sails of the finest silk, and once again he set sail for the fair land of Northumbria.

Warned by her magic powers that Childe Wynd was returning, the witch-queen again climbed the spiral staircase to the topmost room of the main tower which overlooked the grey North Sea, and as soon as she spied the sails of the ship on the horizon, she began to conjure up another storm. But this time her spells failed her; the sea remained calm and grey and the wind was nothing more than a helpful breeze to fill the silken sails and speed the vessel to land.

Scowling with anger, the witch-queen summoned her witch-wives and sent them out in a magic boat with orders to sink Childe Wynd's ship and drown all those who sailed on her—but the witch-wives returned, sullen and angry, crying out that there was rowan wood on the new ship and so their spells were of no use against her or those who sailed in her.

Green fire flashed from the witch-queen's eyes as she tried, for the third time, to prevent Childe Wynd from landing on the yellow sands, and this time she sent a boat with armed men to attack him—but as soon as the men recognised Childe Wynd they laid down their arms and refused to fight, because they knew that he was no raider but the king's son and heir. And Childe Wynd steered his ship to the north of Bamburgh and beached her in Budle Bay, and leaving his men there, he set forth to find the laidley worm in its cave in Spindlestone Heugh.

All around him the countryside was wasted by the fire of the dragon's breath: not a flower was to be seen in the hedgerows, not a leaf on the trees, not a blade of grass in the fields. 'How can it be,' he wondered, 'that this loathsome dragon has thus scorched the countryside and yet it has killed no man?'

71

On he walked until he came to Spindlestone Heugh, and there he saw the dragon asleep, coiled round the foot of the hill. Pulling his sword from its scabbard, he raised it high above his head, so that it flashed in the rays of the setting sun—but at the very moment he was about to bring it down, the dragon awoke and stared at him with sad blue eyes, and then, to his amazement, it spoke.

> O quit thy sword, and bend thy bow,
> And give me kisses three,
> For though I be a poisonous Worm
> No hurt I'll do to thee.

Lowering his sword, Childe Wynd gazed in bewilderment as the dragon spoke again,

> O quit thy sword, and bend thy bow,
> And give me kisses three,
> If I'm not won ere set of sun
> Won shall I never be.

Placing his sword on the ground, Childe Wynd bent one knee and looked long into the sad blue eyes of the dragon, shivering a little at the scaly face and ugly mouth, but now he knew that witchcraft had been at work. Leaning forward, he kissed the laidley worm once, and the creature sighed and tightened its coils round the foot of Spindlestone Heugh; he kissed it twice and it sighed again and began to tremble, so that the entire hill began to shake; as he kissed it for the third time the sun sank in the west and the loathsome dragon vanished and in its place stood his sister, the Lady Margaret.

'Who was it that dared to cast this spell on you and turned the fairest in the whole of Northumbria into a laidley worm?' Childe Wynd cried, throwing his cloak around his sister—but she did not know, and all she could do was put her arms around Childe Wynd and cry for joy that the spell was broken.

'Who was it that dared to cast this spell on my sister Margaret and turned her into a laidley worm?' Childe Wynd asked the country people, who had gathered round to see him slay the dragon and who now marvelled that the Lady Margaret had been found again. But no one knew the answer, and all they could do was to shake their heads and rejoice that the spell was broken and that the laidley worm was no more.

'Who was it that dared to cast this spell on the kindest and gentlest lady in the whole of fair Northumbria?' Childe Wynd asked, as he entered the hall of the royal castle at Bamburgh, with the Lady Margaret by his side. Although the courtiers guessed, they dared not speak for fear of offending the witch-queen and bringing disaster on themselves, and so they shook their heads and said nothing, although they all rejoiced that the Lady Margaret had come back.

Only the old Border chieftain who followed Childe Wynd into the hall had no fear.

'All this has been the work of a witch,' he cried, 'but I shall name no names until you name her for yourself.'

At this the courtiers gave way to right and left and Childe Wynd, with the Lady Margaret on his arm, walked the length of the great hall to where the king and the witch-queen were seated in state on their thrones.

'Margaret!' the king cried, rising and folding his daughter in his arms. 'My lost child, Margaret!'

But the witch-queen shuddered as her eyes met those of Childe Wynd, and the colour fled from her cheeks so that she looked haggard and old.

'It is the queen herself who bewitched my sister, the fairest in all Northumbria, and turned her into a laidley worm,' Childe Wynd cried in ringing tones, and at that moment the witch-queen's magic vanished, so that when the king turned to look at her he realized that what his son had said was indeed true.

Terrified now that her wickedness had been discovered, the

witch-queen shivered and, no longer beautiful, she shrank under the stern gaze of Childe Wynd until she changed into a wrinkled toad, and then she hopped down the stone steps to the kitchen and with a loud cry jumped into the well in the centre of the room and sank to the bottom, and no one ever heard of her again from that day to this.

And all the courtiers and all the servants in the castle, down to the smallest scullery maid and the youngest page, and all the people in the village and in the surrounding countryside rejoiced because Childe Wynd had freed Lady Margaret from the spells of the witch-queen and the Laidley Worm of Spindlestone Heugh no longer existed. And peace reigned throughout the fair land of Northumbria and the king, with the Lady Margaret, his daughter, and Childe Wynd, his son, lived happily and contentedly ever after.

8

THE JI-JALLER BAG

Long ago, an old woman came to live in a village on the banks of the bonny River Tyne. Her name was Dame Clootie.

The men in the village had been happy and well contented with their lot: they worked for the lord of the manor, cared for his sheep and cattle and cultivated his land and thus they provided their families with good homes, warm clothing and plenty to eat —until Dame Clootie came to live on the outskirts of the village, in the cottage with the crooked chimney.

The women in the village had been industrious and cheerful: they baked their own bread and scones and brewed their own ale and saw that their families were warmly clad in winter and properly fed all the year round—until Dame Clootie came to live on the outskirts of the village, in the cottage with the crooked chimney.

The children in the village—well! they were just like any group of children anywhere, in any age: sometimes they were good and sometimes they were naughty, but they were all very happy because their parents loved them and cared for them, and they would laugh and chatter as they played together on the village green—until Dame Clootie came to live in the cottage with the crooked chimney.

One night, as Fair Janet, the shepherd's daughter, sat spinning by the light of the fire, her mother sighed as she looked at the bare shelves of her pantry.

'It was a sad day for us when Dame Clootie came to live in the cottage with the crooked chimney on the edge of Starvecrow Field,' she said. 'Was it our fault that she had been there a week

before anyone in the village knew about it? Why, the very day I heard about it, didn't I hurry over with one of my singin' hinnies —which everyone says are the best in the whole of Northumberland!—and didn't Mistress Margery next door take her a jar of mead and Mistress Agnes opposite a bundle of kindling? And what happened?'

Fair Janet looked sadly at her mother and sighed. Everyone knew what had happened. Those who had brought presents to welcome Dame Clootie were told to bring exactly the same every week: if once they missed, a hen would stop laying or a cow would no longer give milk or a sheep would fall dead on the hillside. As for those who had done nothing to welcome Dame Clootie, they found that their butter would not churn, their husbands returned home from the fields racked with aches and pains, and their children became bad-tempered and quarrelsome, waking in the night and crying because they had earache or toothache.

Only when it was too late did they realize that Dame Clootie was no ordinary old woman, but a malicious and bad-tempered witch.

They wore themselves out taking gifts to appease her, but they knew that once a week Dame Clootie set out for the market at Newcastle, and while they went cold and hungry, she sold the eggs and butter and milk, the wool and the cloth which they had been forced to give her, and in exchange she received round, shining golden guineas, which she put in a bag underneath her apron and carried home and hid somewhere in the cottage with the crooked chimney.

'It was a sad day for us when Dame Clootie came to live in the cottage with the crooked chimney on the edge of Starvecrow Field,' the shepherd's wife repeated. 'Because of what we have to give her, each year we grow poorer and poorer; more and more of us fall ill and half the children do not get enough to eat now.'

'Don't cry, Mammy,' Fair Janet said softly. 'Some day Dame

Clootie will be sorry for all the mischief she has worked and the unhappiness she has caused.'

But the very next day—which was a Saturday—Dame Clootie hobbled down to the village, her face dark and scowling.

'Don't shut your doors on me,' she cried, as all the goodwives hurried into their homes, to close the windows and bolt the doors. 'I have come to tell you that I am tired of looking after myself in the cottage with the twisted chimney. At my time of life I am entitled to a little peace. I need a little servant-girl to keep my cottage clean and tidy, and sweep out every corner of the kitchen, and light my fires and prepare my meals, and scour the pots until they shine so brightly that I can see my face in them.'

When the goodwives heard this, they trembled, because although they were poor, none of them wanted to send her daughter to be a servant-maid to the witch. Just at that moment, however, a travelling tinker happened to be passing through the village. He knew all about Dame Clootie's weekly visits to the market at Newcastle, and the goods which she exchanged for golden guineas.

'I've just the girl for you,' he called out. 'My daughter, Clever Kate. She's strong and clean and willing, and when it comes to scouring pots, there's no one to beat her in the whole of Northumberland.'

'Send her up tomorrow,' Dame Clootie said. 'She'll eat with me at the kitchen table, and at night she'll sleep underneath it, and if she still pleases me after seven years and a day, I'll pay her one shining, golden guinea.' And she hobbled back to her cottage while the tinker went off rubbing his hands, and the goodwives gathered together and wondered what would come of it all, because everyone knew that he was the biggest rogue in the whole of Northumberland and that nothing was safe when Clever Kate was around.

The next morning, Clever Kate set out for Dame Clootie's cottage. She had washed her face and hands in the millstream, and combed her hair with a comb she had taken from the sill of an open window: the red dress she was wearing was one she had found the previous day hanging on the washing-line behind one of the cottages, and her green cloak belonged to the blacksmith's daughter, who had hung it on a bush because it made her too hot while she was playing Jack Jump Over the Water.

Just as she reached the cottage, Blackmalkin, Dame Clootie's cat, sidled out and rubbed itself against her leg.

'Clever Kate,' he said, 'pour me some milk in my own white saucer,' and he began to purr contentedly.

'Pour it yourself!' Kate answered. 'I haven't come to look after a cat.' She pushed him aside with her foot, and knocked on the door, and the cat looked at her and stopped purring.

When Dame Clootie opened the door and saw Clever Kate, she was well pleased that the girl looked strong and healthy and able to work hard.

'Come in!' she said. 'You are to keep my cottage clean and tidy, and sweep out every corner of the kitchen, and light my fires and prepare my meals, and scour the pots so brightly that I can see my face in them.'

'That I will do,' said Clever Kate, and stepping aside she picked up the broom and set to work, while Blackmalkin the cat sat on a chair and stared at her but made not the slightest sound.

'There is one thing I want you to remember,' Dame Clootie continued. 'You must be sure never to put your broom up the crooked chimney.'

'So that's where she keeps it,' thought Clever Kate, as she nodded her head and went on sweeping. All day she worked and in the evening, when Dame Clootie saw her reflection in the polished pans, she was well contented with her serving-maid and hobbled upstairs to bed.

'I might as well have my sleep,' thought Clever Kate, and she curled up under the kitchen table, but at the first cock-crow she wakened, fetched Dame Clootie's broom, and pushed it up the

chimney as far as she could reach. Down fell a big bag, bulging
with shining, golden guineas! Laughing to herself, Clever Kate
picked up the bag and hurried out of the cottage, stopping only
to put on the green cloak which she had taken from the bush
while the blacksmith's daughter was playing Jack Jump Over the
Water.

Through Starvecrow Field she ran until she came to a gate at
the far side.

'Pretty maid,' the gate said, 'will you open me, for I have not
been opened for many a year?'

But Kate tossed her black hair and shook her head.

'Open yourself,' she answered. 'I have no time to open you.'
And putting one hand on the fence, she leaped lightly over and
ran on.

Presently she came to a cow standing in the middle of a field of
green grass and yellow buttercups.

'Pretty maid,' the cow said, 'will you stop and milk me, for I
have not been milked for many a year?'

But Kate tossed her black hair and shook her head.

'Milk yourself,' she answered. 'I have no time to milk you.'

And she ran on until she came to a mill by the banks of the
bonny Tyne, and there three ducks swam idly and dived for
worms in the rich mud of the river bed.

'Pretty maid,' the mill said, 'will you turn me for I have not
been turned for many a year?' But Kate tossed her black hair and
shook her head.

'Turn yourself,' she answered. 'I have no time to turn you.'

By this time she was in a very bad temper: the bag of golden
guineas which she was carrying was growing heavier and heavier,
she had run so hard that she was out of breath and had risen so
early that she was terribly sleepy.

'Why should I do all the work?' she asked herself. 'I found
Dame Clootie's money and I've carried it so far, now my father
can come and fetch it.' And she hid the bag in the mill-hopper

(which is the big trough where the corn is placed, before it is passed to the mill to be ground into flour) and ran off to her father to tell him how clever she had been.

When the cock crowed for the third time, Dame Clootie awoke and went downstairs to find the floor unswept, the fire unlit, and the soot from the crooked chimney all over the hearth, and she knew straightaway that Clever Kate had put her broom up the chimney and found her money.

'She shall pay for this!' she muttered, and she hobbled off across Starvecrow Field until she came to the gate at the far side.

'Gate o' mine, gate o' mine,' she cried, 'have you seen a maid o' mine, with a ji-jaller bag and a long leather bag, with all the money in it that I ever had?'

And the gate said, 'Farther on.'

Through the field of green grass and yellow buttercups she hobbled until she came to the cow which was standing there.

'Cow o' mine, cow o' mine,' she cried, 'have you seen a maid o' mine, with a ji-jaller bag and a long leather bag, with all the money in it that I ever had?'

And the cow said, 'Farther on.'

On she hobbled until she came to the mill by the banks of the bonny Tyne and the three ducks which swam idly and dived for worms among the rich mud.

'Mill o' mine, mill o' mine,' she cried, 'have you seen a maid o' mine, with a ji-jaller bag and a long leather bag, with all the money in it that I ever had?'

And the mill said, 'In the mill hopper.'

Plunging her hands into the corn, Dame Clootie found the bag which still bulged with her precious golden guineas, and she set off again, back to her cottage, and once more she hid it up the crooked chimney.

As for Clever Kate, when she returned to the mill with her father, the tinker, and realized that Dame Clootie had got there before her, she was very frightened because she knew what trouble the old woman could cause, and so she and her father packed their things there and then and set off across the bridge which spanned the bonny River Tyne, and neither of them was ever seen again in Northumberland.

The following Saturday, Dame Clootie hobbled down again to the village.

'Don't shut your doors on me,' she cried. 'I need another little servant-girl who will keep my cottage clean and tidy and scour the pots until they shine so brightly that I can see my face in them.'

This time there was no dishonest tinker to send his daughter, and Dame Clootie's face grew dark with anger, and just as she was going to ill-wish everyone in the village, Fair Janet, the shepherd's daughter, stepped forward.

'I will be your little servant-girl,' she said gently, 'and I will work for you for seven years and a day for one golden guinea, but you must promise to let me come home every Sunday morning so that I can go to the little stone church on the top of the hill with my Mammy and my Daddy.'

Dame Clootie nodded her head and hobbled back home, with Fair Janet following behind, and when they got to the cottage, Blackmalkin, the cat, sidled out and rubbed himself against the girl's legs.

'Fair Janet,' he said, 'pour me some milk in my own white saucer.'

'Willingly,' answered Fair Janet, and she filled his saucer with milk.

'There is one thing I want you to remember,' Dame Clootie said. 'You must be sure never to put your broom up the crooked chimney.' But the cat purred so loudly when Dame Clootie said 'never' that Fair Janet thought she had told her to be sure to sweep the chimney, and so she smiled and nodded her head and began to brush the floor vigorously.

At the first cock-crow the next morning she awoke.

'Today I must go back to my Mammy and my Daddy, to go with them to the little stone church on the top of the hill,' she said to herself, 'but first I must sweep the crooked chimney.' And she fetched Dame Clootie's broom and pushed it up the chimney as far as she could reach, and down fell the bag, bulging with shining, golden guineas.

Looking at the money, Fair Janet thought of all the men and women in the village who had gone cold and all the children who had gone hungry, to satisfy the greed of Dame Clootie.

'I must ask my Mammy and my Daddy what I should do,' she said, and she picked up the bag and hurried through the field until she came to the gate.

'Pretty maid,' said the gate, 'will you stop and open me, for I have not been opened for many a year?'

'Willingly,' answered Fair Janet, and she opened the gate and hurried through.

Presently she came to the cow which was standing in the field of green grass and yellow buttercups.

'Pretty maid,' the cow said, 'will you stop and milk me for I have not been milked for many a year?'

'Willingly,' answered Fair Janet, and she sat down and milked the cow, and then she hurried on until she came to the mill by the banks of the bonny River Tyne.

'Pretty maid,' the mill said, 'will you turn me for I have not been turned for many a year?'

'Willingly,' answered Fair Janet, and she turned the mill and then she ran as fast as she could to her home.

At the third cock-crow, Dame Clootie awoke and went downstairs to find soot all over the hearth, and she knew straightaway that Fair Janet had put her broom up the chimney and found her money.

'She shall pay for this,' she muttered, and she hurried off across the field.

'Gate o' mine, gate o' mine,' she cried, 'have you seen a maid

84

o' mine, with a ji-jaller bag and a long leather bag, with all the money in it that I ever had?'

But the gate said nothing because Fair Janet had opened it.

And the cow said nothing because Fair Janet had milked her.

And when Dame Clootie reached the mill and asked her question, and the mill said nothing because Fair Janet had turned it, then at that very moment she realized that she had lost all her magic powers and had forgotten all her spells; now, instead of being a wicked witch, she was only a poor and helpless old woman whom no one could possibly love.

As it happened, she was luckier than she deserved. When Fair Janet and her Mammy and her Daddy went to the little stone church on the top of the hill, they took with them the ji-jaller bag and all the money that Dame Clootie ever had, and they gave it to the priest, and he divided it out equally among the men and women of the village because, of course, it really had belonged to them. But when the villagers heard what had happened to Dame Clootie, and how she was no longer a witch but just a poor and helpless old woman, they gave her some of the money from the ji-jaller bag for herself, and from time to time Fair Janet would take her little presents of eggs or butter or milk or one of her Mammy's singin' hinnies, and so Dame Clootie spent the rest of her days quietly with Blackmalkin in the cottage with the crooked chimney on the edge of Starvecrow Field.

9

YOUNG POLLARD AND THE BRAWN
OF BISHOP AUCKLAND

A long time ago, when a great deal of the north of England was covered by dense forests in which roamed all kinds of wild and dangerous animals, a ferocious Brawn spread fear and terror among all those who lived near Bishop Auckland, in the County of Durham.

This wild boar was the most fearsome creature to look at: twice as big as any ordinary pig, its body was covered with thick, woolly hair and coarse black bristles; from the sides of its mouth curved cruel tusks, and mean little eyes peered to right and left, and for all its size and heaviness, it could run faster than any man.

The Brawn lived by itself, feeding on the crops sown by the peasants and farmers and destroying what it could not eat: it hated all the other animals that lived in the forests, but most of all it hated human beings, and at night it would lurk in the undergrowth, watching its chance to attack and kill some tired, unsuspecting peasant as he returned home from work.

Most of the people who lived in that district were the tenants and retainers of the rich and powerful Bishop of Durham, who lived in Auckland Castle, and finally, so terrified were they of the Brawn, that they sent a petition to the Bishop, asking if he could help them because no one dared stir abroad after sunset and even in the daytime they went in fear of their lives.

The Bishop agreed that something must be done to protect his people, and he announced that a princely reward would be given to anyone brave enough and clever enough to slay the Brawn.

The young men in the neighbourhood, however, shook their heads, remembering how more than one gallant knight had ridden up from the South, boasting of the dragons and other dreaded creatures he had slain, but none had returned from the dark forests where the Brawn roamed in search of prey. What was the good of a princely reward, they whispered among themselves, if they weren't alive to claim it?

The only person interested in the Bishop's offer was a young man called Pollard: he came of an old and distinguished family, but he was the youngest son and he knew that he would inherit neither lands nor money and so would have to make his own way in the world.

'A princely reward would do me very nicely,' he thought, 'but as I mean to stay alive to claim it, it is important that I plan very carefully what I must do.

'The Brawn has killed simple peasants and farmers who were no fighters, but it has also killed valiant knights who were properly armed and trained both to attack and defend. This means it is either stronger than the strongest man or else it is more cunning. Perhaps, indeed, it is both. It seems to me that the first thing I must do is to learn all about the Brawn and its habits, so that I can first match cunning with cunning and then strength with strength.'

Leaving his sword and armour at home and his horse in its stable, and with only bread and cheese in his wallet to feed him, young Pollard set off the next morning for the woods where the Brawn lurked: with his ears alert for the slightest sound, his eyes keen to note the smallest sign, he followed the tracks made by the creature through the forests and the countryside. Sometimes he watched by day and sometimes by night and so careful and cunning was he that the Brawn had no idea he was being spied on.

At the end of a month, young Pollard thought that he knew as much about the savage monster as he did about himself.

The Brawn was even bigger and uglier than he had imagined possible and it was far stronger and swifter than any boar he had ever known. It was a greedy feeder, never stopping when it had had enough, and though it ate all kinds of crops and plants, what it preferred above all else were the ripe nuts which fell from the beech trees and lay thickly on the ground. Its lair, young Pollard had discovered, was in the heart of Etherley Dene, where its favourite beech trees flourished and where it could eat its fill after roaming the countryside all night and leaving in its wake a trail of damage and destruction.

Now young Pollard knew what he must do.

The next evening, arming himself with his falchion—a short, curved sword something like a sickle—and mounting his mare, Jennet, he rode to a farmhouse not far from Etherley Dene: here he left his mare and went on foot to the Dene. The Brawn, he knew, would be roaming the countryside and would not return until dawn to eat its last meal and to sleep in its lair. Previously he had noted the tallest and strongest beech tree nearest to the creature's den, and now he climbed up this tree and shook down a great heap of beech nuts so that they were scattered temptingly on the ground, in full view of the returning Brawn.

After that there was nothing for him to do but to find a comfortable fork in the branches, high up in the tree, where he was well hidden by the leaves, and wait as patiently as he could.

Just as the pale light of the false dawn stole across the eastern sky, his ears caught the sound of the Brawn making its way along the track, snorting and grunting and rootling for food among the fallen leaves and the bracken. Suddenly the noise stopped and young Pollard knew that the creature had spied the beech nuts: the next moment it began to devour them, grunting and snuffling as though it could not gobble them up fast enough. Young Pollard thought he had shaken down enough beechmast for a whole herd of boars, but now it seemed as though the Brawn would never be

satisfied. All the time, even though he had a cramp in one leg and his sword arm ached from gripping the branch which was supporting him, young Pollard dared not move a muscle, because he knew how keen was the creature's hearing, how suspicious it was of the slightest movement near it.

At last every nut was eaten and the boar, grunting with satisfaction, turned heavily towards its lair: with a loud snort it lowered itself to the ground, turned on to one side and closed its eyes, worn out by its long night's hunting and the huge meal it had just eaten.

When he was sure the Brawn was asleep, young Pollard flexed his arms and legs carefully to restore the circulation and then, very quietly, he climbed down the tree. Drawing his falchion, he crept towards the Brawn's lair, hoping to kill it before it awakened, but the creature's hearing was even keener than he had realized.

With a horrible snorting it lumbered to its feet and charged straight at young Pollard. Nimbly the young man leapt to one side, aware now that no matter how tired the creature might be after feasting, it was still a cruel and cunning fighter.

Throughout the whole, long day young Pollard and the Brawn fought on equal terms in Etherley Dene, but as the sun went down and the stars came out one by one, young Pollard began to tire and the boar drove him deeper and deeper into the Dene. But when the bell in the distant church in Bishop Auckland tolled midnight, the young man rallied and now it was the turn of the Brawn to weaken and retreat. All through the starlit night the duel continued, but just as the first rays of the rising sun tinged the tops of the trees, young Pollard roused himself to his last and greatest effort and with a powerful swing of his falchion he slew the Brawn.

Wounded himself and utterly exhausted, he looked down on the fearsome creature which had wrought such havoc: he had no strength left to go back for his mare and ride to the Bishop with the good news: all he wanted to do was to lie down and sleep. With a weary sigh he stooped, cut out the boar's tongue and put it in his wallet, and then he stumbled across to a bracken covered bank, curled up, and the next moment was sound asleep.

All day he slept. So tired was he and so deep his sleep that he never heard the birds singing in the branches above, the rabbits running round the foot of the bank or the vixen, velvet-padded, passing within a few inches of his head.

Nor did he hear the traveller who passed by late in the afternoon and reined his horse as he stared in amazement at the sight of the fearsome Brawn lying by the edge of the wood.

'This must be the very same creature which has plagued the countryside for years,' the traveller said to himself, and because he could not see young Pollard asleep in the bracken, he thought some other animal must have fought with the Brawn and killed it. 'Why shouldn't I claim the reward?' he thought, and dismounting from his horse, he cut off the boar's head, tied it to his saddle, and rejoicing in his luck, set off at a gallop for the palace at Bishop Auckland.

It was not long after this that young Pollard awoke, stretched himself and decided that after washing in the nearby stream he would be fit to claim his reward; but when he got to his feet and saw the headless Brawn, his heart sank and he was filled with dismay.

'I should have gone straight to the Bishop this morning,' he cried, 'and claimed the reward then. But I was too tired. No man could fight all day and all night as I did and not be exhausted. But now it seems that I have planned and fought for nothing, for some imposter will take my place. And yet perhaps it is not too late. Perhaps I can convince the Bishop that it was really I who slew the creature.'

Hurrying to the farmhouse where he had left Jennet, his mare, he mounted and rode straight for Auckland Castle.

'I must see the Bishop,' he cried, when the sentry challenged him. 'My name is young Pollard and I have come to claim the reward because I have slain the Brawn.'

'That's a likely story,' the sentry said. 'Why, at this very moment there is a traveller with his lordship, and he's the one who killed the Brawn because he's got the head to prove it.'

But young Pollard coaxed and argued and pleaded until, for the sake of peace, the sentry let him pass and one of the servants led him to the Great Hall where the Bishop was sitting in state. In front of him stood the traveller, holding up the Brawn's head for all to see, while servants and retainers gathered round, talking and exclaiming at the fearsomeness of the boar, and admiring and envying the hero who claimed to have slain it.

Just as young Pollard entered the hall, the Bishop raised his hand for silence and then turned to the traveller.

'You have freed the countryside of a terrible scourge,' he said, 'and for your valour you shall be well rewarded.'

'Wait, my lord!' young Pollard cried, shaking off the servants who tried to hold him back and striding down to the far end of the hall where the Bishop was seated. 'It was I who killed the Brawn and not this traveller.' And he went on to explain how exhausted he had been after the long fight and how he had fallen asleep and slept all day.

'That's a likely story!' the traveller said with a sneer. 'It was I who killed the Brawn and to prove it I've brought the head for all to see.'

'The head proves nothing except that you cut it off,' young Pollard replied, and opening his wallet, he took out the tongue and flung it down on the floor beside the boar's head. 'That is my proof that it was I who slew the Brawn!'

Slowly the Bishop stroked his beard, looking first from the tongue to the head, and then from young Pollard to the traveller, and because he was very wise and could read men's characters in their faces, he knew which of the two was telling the truth, but he knew also that all those in the Great Hall had to be convinced.

'Open the boar's mouth and see if it lacks a tongue,' he commanded. As the servants hurried forward to obey, the traveller, realizing that the truth would out, turned and slunk out of the hall, and rode away from the Castle as fast as he could, leaving young Pollard to tell the whole story of how for a month he had studied the Brawn's habits and had chosen to attack it when it was tired from wandering about and drowsy from over-eating.

'Remarkable!' the Bishop said, looking at the young man with admiration. 'You certainly deserve the rich reward which I offered. Now I will tell you what it is. As it happens, I am just going in to dinner: if you return to me when I have finished eating, I will give you all the land that you have been able to ride around.' And he signed to his servants to open the doors which led into the dining-room.

'How long does it take the Bishop to eat his dinner?' young Pollard asked one of the retainers as he returned to the courtyard.

'Generally about an hour,' the servant answered, 'but I could see that he liked you and your courage, and because he will want you to have a generous reward, I am sure he will make his meal last an hour and a quarter tonight.'

'Thank you,' young Pollard said, and mounting his mare he rode off in a very leisurely fashion.

The Bishop, as the retainer had thought, ate rather more slowly than was his wont so that it took him an hour and a half to finish his meal that evening.

'Has the young man yet returned?' he asked one of the footmen as he emptied his glass of wine.

'Returned? My lord, he has been waiting in the hall this last three quarters of an hour or more.'

'Indeed?' A pleased smile lit the Bishop's face. 'Obviously a modest young man as well as a brave one. I thought that the moment I set eyes on him, but then everyone knows I am a pretty good judge of character.' And with a slow and stately tread he made his way back to the Great Hall, and as the young man fell on one knee, the Bishop smiled again and extended his hand so that young Pollard might kiss the jewelled ring which flashed and sparkled in the candle-light.

'You might have ridden twice as far in the time I allowed you,' the Bishop said graciously.

'I know, my lord,' young Pollard said with a modest little smile.

'A most unusual and humble young man,' the Bishop murmured. 'And how far did you ride?'

'Once round your lordship's own castle,' young Pollard answered.

The smile vanished from the Bishop's face.

'Once round—my castle?' he said.

'Yes, my lord.'

'Once round my castle!' the Bishop repeated again. Staring at young Pollard he sank heavily into his chair, and then suddenly he threw back his head and roared with laughter, and all the servants and footmen and retainers turned to one another and laughed and shook their heads and laughed again.

'I might have known,' the Bishop gasped, wiping away the tears of mirth which trickled down his cheeks, 'that a man who could match the cunning of the Brawn with a cunning of his own would be much too clever for a simple Bishop.' Sighing, he looked thoughtfully at young Pollard. 'And so you lay claim to my castle and all my furniture and goods and chattels?'

'Your lordship did make a promise,' young Pollard reminded him.

'True, true. But perhaps there are certain aspects of the situation which you have not fully considered. The castle, for instance. It is abominably cold and chilly, even in summer, and if you don't suffer from rheumatism and chilblains now, you certainly will if you have to live here. And then there's the upkeep of the place. It costs a fortune to keep it in good repair. And then there are the servants—expecting to be paid every year for the work they do, and if you saw the bills I get for their food . . . !' The Bishop threw up his hands and looked faint at the mere thought of these. 'What a younger son really needs is land of his own.'

Turning from young Pollard, the Bishop beckoned to one of his retainers.

'Bring me a map of all the lands in Durham which belong to the Bishop County Palatine,' he ordered, and while the servant hurried off the Bishop hummed a little and inspected his ring and stole occasional glances at the silent young man before him.

Quickly the retainer returned, and at a sign from the Bishop, unrolled the parchment and exhibited the map, which showed the great Abbey at Durham and the castle at Bishop Auckland and all the lands which belonged to the church. The Bishop hummed a little louder.

'As I was saying, what a younger son really needs is land of his own. Here for instance'—a bejewelled hand indicated land not far from the castle itself—'we have rich meadows, fertile pasture and well-timbered forest, with an excellent site on this hill for a gentleman to build himself a modern house.'

Raising one eyebrow, the Bishop looked at young Pollard, and young Pollard, after studying the map a moment longer, looked at the Bishop and nodded his head. And they both smiled. And then they both laughed. And everyone in the Great Hall joined in the merriment.

And that was how the Bishop redeemed his castle in return for a fine estate, and even to this day the land which he gave the young man is called Pollard's lands, and so proud were young Pollard's family of the way he fought and killed the fearsome Brawn of Bishop Auckland, that for their family crest they took a strong right arm holding a falchion.

10

MARY-ANN AND THE CAULD LAD
OF HYLTON

A long time ago, when there were no coal or lead mines and no big towns in Durham County, when the River Wear flowed through thick forests and fine pastures and by many a fine castle, there lived a little orphan called Mary-Ann.

She knew that once she must have had a mother and a father because she could remember being hugged and kissed and loved, but it was such a long time ago that sometimes she wondered if perhaps it was just something she had dreamed.

Not long after her parents died, her uncle, a poor wood-cutter who lived in Weardale, had taken her home with him.

'Here, wife,' he said. 'We have so many children of our own that one more won't make any difference.' And he handed Mary-Ann over and went out to sharpen his axe for his work next day.

Now the wood-cutter's wife was not an unkind woman, but she had to work so hard to feed and clothe her own family and her husband made so little money with his wood-cutting, that she really did not want Mary-Ann, and as the years passed and her family kept on increasing, she wanted her less and less.

Poor Mary-Ann! She worked hard to try to please the wood-cutter's wife, scrubbing and cleaning the little cottage, looking after the babies and putting them to bed, playing with the older children and mending their clothes and even going out at harvest time to help in the fields, but it seemed as though the very sight of Mary-Ann upset her. When there wasn't enough to eat in the house, she grudged Mary-Ann the poor scraps that were her meal.

One night, too tired to sleep because of all the work she had done that day and because the younger children had been particularly naughty and the older ones had teased and pinched her, Mary-Ann was lying on the straw which was her bed in the scullery when she heard the wood-cutter talking in the kitchen to his wife. He did not bother to lower his voice because he was sure Mary-Ann was asleep.

'If there isn't enough food, it's not my fault,' he said. 'I work twice as hard as any man I know and give you every penny I earn.'

'There would be enough if there was one mouth less,' his wife answered sharply.

'I suppose you're talking about Mary-Ann again. But you can't just put her out. After all she is the daughter of my own sister.'

'No one is talking about putting her out, husband. For years we have looked after her and given her a good home. Now she is old enough to go away to work and keep herself.'

'And where in Weardale is a little lass like her to find work?' the wood-cutter demanded.

'She doesn't need to find it,' his wife said triumphantly. 'I've done that for her.'

'You have? Where?'

'At Hylton Castle. I saw the housekeeper at the market today and it's all arranged. She's to be the second under-kitchen-maid and you're to take her to the castle on Sunday.'

To work at Hylton Castle! Mary-Ann could scarcely believe her ears. A castle! It sounded too good to be true. And so excited was she at the very thought that she did not hear the protests the wood-cutter made or the doubts he expressed about sending anyone to work in a place like Hylton Castle.

The next day, when the wood-cutter's wife told Mary-Ann what had been arranged, the little orphan smiled and immediately set to work to wash the few, poor clothes which she possessed and to see that they were neatly darned and mended and tied up in a bundle so that she could carry them. The following day, which was Sunday, she kissed all the children good-bye and set off with the wood-cutter to walk the ten miles to the Castle where she was to live and work and keep herself.

When at last they arrived at the Castle, Mary-Ann's eyes opened wide. Never had she seen such a magnificent place. Overcome, she stared at the massive stone walls and towers, the narrow windows, the sculptured men-at-arms placed on the turrets as though on guard for ever.

'Here you are,' the wood-cutter said, giving Mary-Ann a penny piece. 'Work hard and obey the housekeeper, and if you say your prayers every night, no matter what may happen in the Castle, you will be all right.' And turning abruptly, he strode off, leaving Mary-Ann to find her own way round to the back of the Castle where the servants lived.

The housekeeper, who was plump and hard-working and efficient, bustled forward, her keys jingling from the long chain clipped round her waist.

'What a poor, skinny little thing you are,' she said, gazing doubtfully at Mary-Ann. 'The wood-cutter's wife said you were a good worker who never grumbled and never ate much.'

'That's true, Ma'am,' Mary-Ann said, dropping a curtsey, terrified that she would lose the job in this castle which was finer and more magnificent than anything she had ever imagined. 'In fact, I hardly eat anything at all.'

'That's exactly what I was thinking,' the housekeeper said, and taking a large wooden platter she put on it a ham bone which still had plenty of fat meat and plenty of lean, a couple of chicken wings, a generous helping of pease pudding and a thick slice of rye bread. 'Now sit down here at the table,' she said, 'and don't get up until there's nothing left on the platter but bones. I'll have no starving lasses working under me.'

'Why, it's like living in Heaven,' Mary-Ann said to the first under-kitchen-maid that night, as they climbed upstairs to their

bedroom in one of the attics. 'Such wonderful food and a real bedroom to sleep in!'

'You don't think she does all this just because she's tender-hearted, do you?' the first under-kitchen-maid asked scornfully. 'Don't you know that she's getting desperate for servants? The only ones who will stay here are the ones who are too old to get other jobs. None of the others stay more than a few months. I don't get paid until the end of the year, but if things go on as they have been doing, I'm running away without my wages.'

'What do you mean? What things have been going on?' Mary-Ann asked, very mystified.

'Just you wait and you'll find out for yourself,' the first under-kitchen-maid answered, and without bothering to take off any of her clothes, she jumped into bed, rolled the blankets round her and fell fast asleep.

'Time to worry when there's something to worry about,' Mary-Ann said to herself as she undressed and put on her old, patched nightgown; kneeling down beside the bed, she said her prayers, with a special prayer for the housekeeper who had fed her, and then, well content, she too fell fast asleep.

Now, although she was used to rising early to help the wood-cutter's wife look after the children, Mary-Ann was so tired after her long walk to the Castle and the excitement of her first day there, that she was still half asleep as she made her way down the back staircase to the kitchen, the next morning, to clean out the range and set and light the fire.

Behind her clattered the first under-kitchen-maid, and behind her came the scullion, a tall, gangling lad who never seemed to have a word to say for himself, who worked all the time even when no one was watching him, and who was the butt of the other servants because no matter how much he was teased, he would just smile and refuse to fight or even to lose his temper.

'Goodness!' Mary-Ann cried, as she saw the big kitchen which she and the first under-kitchen-maid had tidied last thing before they went to bed the previous night.

'Goodness!' she cried again, rubbing her eyes and looking a second time. 'Who did this?'

The shining copper pans and bowls, which last night had hung on their hooks on the wall, were scattered all over the floor: the long wooden table, where the servants sat in order of rank and priority, was turned upside down: the ashes from the fire had been shovelled into the ovens.

'You see!' the first under-kitchen-maid said triumphantly. 'That's why none of the servants will stay. *He's* been at it again.'

'Who is he?' Mary-Ann asked.

'The Cauld Lad of Hylton, of course. He's a horrible, wicked Brownie and he comes here every night and undoes all the work we've done and makes the most awful mess—as though there wasn't enough work for us already.'

The scullion said nothing. He just set to work picking up the pots and bowls and putting them aside to be washed again, and then, very carefully, he began to clear the ashes out of the ovens.

'Oh, well! It's no good standing here doing nothing,' Mary-Ann said, and she too started to work, so that by the time the under-cook had come down the kitchen was tidy, the copper pots gleamed on the wall and the fire was burning brightly.

It was a wonderful castle and she was the luckiest girl in the world to work in it, Mary-Ann thought, as the days passed. Perhaps the housekeeper was kind to her because so many of the servants were leaving, but the point was that she was nice—and far kinder than the wood-cutter's wife had ever been. Often the scullion helped her too, showing her the easiest way to do a job or helping her to carry some very heavy load, and Mary-Ann hoped that some day as well as smiling at her, he might actually speak to her.

There was no doubt, however, that the Cauld Lad did increase the work and make things difficult, so that tempers were lost in the kitchen far more easily than they should have been, and Mary-Ann found herself thinking about the Brownie very often.

She was used to children, to their naughtiness and rages, their tempers and spitefulness, and so she didn't complain as much as the other servants when they came down in the morning to find the contents of the linen cupboard had been thrown down the stairs, the books in the library had been piled up in the corridor or the treacle poured into the flour bin. Yes, she would agree, the Cauld Lad was naughty, and she would hurry away to clean up the mess and put things straight—and always she would find that the quiet scullion was there before her.

'They wouldn't complain so loudly if they knew as much about children as I do,' she said to the scullion, thinking of the times the older boys had pulled her hair and pinched and slapped her until she cried, the way the younger ones had kicked her and screamed and run away whenever she asked them to do anything they didn't want to do.

The quiet scullion nodded his head.

'And yet they could be so kind and loving sometimes,' Mary-Ann added, thinking of how the older boys had mended her shoes and made her a sledge for Christmas and helped her light the fire in the morning, and how the little ones had put their arms round her neck and cuddled up to her when she told them fairy stories at bed-time. 'They were only naughty when they were bored or when they thought no-one loved them.'

Again the quiet scullion nodded his head.

'It's almost disheartening,' the housekeeper said, a few days later, as she and the butler were talking together. 'I always reckoned to train my servants properly right from the first day, but this Cauld Lad just makes nonsense of all I say.'

'And of all *I* say,' the butler agreed.

'If we leave the kitchen tidy, the dishes washed and the silver cleaned, he untidies everything.'

'But if we leave the place untidy,' the butler said, 'he does all the work and leaves the place spick and span. I don't suppose,' he continued thoughtfully, 'we could get rid of the servants and let the Cauld Lad run the Castle for us? He does the work better than any of the menservants, when he has a mind to it—apart from my scullion, of course.'

'Better than my women servants,' the housekeeper agreed. 'Apart from my second under-kitchen-maid, who will be first under-kitchen-maid as soon as the present one makes up her mind and runs away.

'But I don't think getting rid of the servants would be a good idea. That Brownie has a peculiar sense of humour. Maybe that's just what he'd like us to do and then he'd stop doing any work and you and I would find we'd have to run the whole castle ourselves.'

'Impossible!' the butler said.

'Quite,' the housekeeper agreed. 'In which case, it seems to me that the only thing left is for us to get rid of the Cauld Lad.'

'How?' the butler asked.

'Quite!' the housekeeper agreed, wrinkling her brow and thinking very hard.

All that evening she thought, and all the next day, but she could arrive at no solution, and so in the end she decided to summon all the servants to a meeting in the kitchen and to ask if anyone had any idea how to persuade the Brownie to leave Hylton Castle.

First she looked hopefully at the oldest and wisest servants, but they shook their heads and shrugged their shoulders; and then she looked at the younger ones, but they had no suggestions to offer, and at last she looked at Mary-Ann and the quiet scullion.

'Perhaps he has some reason for being here,' Mary-Ann suggested. 'Has anyone ever asked him why he plays such tricks?'

The housekeeper looked at the butler. Not only had no one ever spoken to the Cauld Lad, no one had even seen him.

'Tonight,' the butler announced firmly, 'one of us will stay up and hide behind that screen in the corner and will report what the

Cauld Lad does and what he looks like and whether it's any good trying to reason with him.'

Everyone agreed that this was a splendid plan, but no one seemed at all keen to stay up and spy on the Cauld Lad. At length, just when the butler was thinking he'd have to do it himself, the quiet scullion spoke.

'I'll do it,' he said, and everyone got such a shock to hear him speak that they forgot to thank him and tell him how brave he was, but they did remind him that Brownies were queer creatures and as like as not the Cauld Lad would turn him into a wooden stool or a quacking duck.

'I'll stay with you,' Mary-Ann whispered, as the other servants went off to their beds.

'Aren't you frightened of Brownies?' the scullion asked, and Mary-Ann was just going to say that she wasn't frightened of anything when she changed her mind.

'Not if I'm with you,' she said, and the scullion's face went very red, though he looked extremely pleased.

The candles were carefully extinguished and only the leaping flames from the logs in the big fireplace lit the kitchen and were reflected in the copper pans and bowls, which hung, each according to its size, on the opposite wall.

Silently Mary-Ann and the scullion waited behind the screen, and just as the last grain of sand trickled from the upper half of the hour-glass at midnight a slim little figure dressed in shabby brown clothes slipped into the room and sat, cross-legged, in front of the fire, warming his hands. Presently he heaved a long deep sigh, and then swaying slightly from side to side, he began to sing a sad little song:

> Wae's me, wae's me,
> The acorn's not yet
> Fallen from the tree,
> That's to grow the wood,

That's to make the cradle,
That's to rock the bairn,
That's to grow the man,
That's to lay me!

When he had finished singing, he sighed again, and getting to his feet, he looked round the kitchen wearily. 'Just as though' (as Mary-Ann told the housekeeper afterwards) 'he was a little boy who didn't know what to do with himself but knew that he had to do something to live up to his reputation.'

Spying the kettle on the hob, the Brownie tilted it until the water ran out on to the glowing logs, which hissed and spat and sent out clouds of steam that filled the whole kitchen, and when they had cleared away, the Cauld Lad had gone.

'You should have told me you were going to stay up,' the housekeeper scolded, when next morning Mary-Ann told her all that had happened.

'I didn't know myself until everyone had gone to bed,' Mary-Ann answered. 'But now that I've seen the Cauld Lad, I don't think it would be any good trying to talk to him. He's dreadfully unhappy. You can tell that by the way he sighs and by the look on his little face. I think that someone's put a spell on him and it can't be broken until someone makes him really happy.'

'But how could we do that?' the housekeeper asked.

'Give him a new suit of clothes,' the scullion said, looking at his own patched jacket and shrunken hose, which had belonged—a long time ago—to a much smaller scullion.

'A splendid idea!' the butler agreed, thinking that perhaps the scullion deserved a new livery because he was such a willing and hard-working lad.

'You must tell me the measurements,' the housekeeper said to Mary-Ann, 'and I shall make it myself. What colour do you think the suit should be?'

'Red,' said Mary-Ann.

'Green,' said the scullion.

'Red cloak and hood, green hose and jerkin,' the butler said briskly.

'I'll do it today,' the housekeeper promised. 'Mary-Ann, look in my button-box and find me six buttons as red as a cherry and six as green as a holly leaf, and when you have finished your work in the kitchen, you can come and sew them on the Cauld Lad's new suit.'

Twenty minutes before midnight the suit was finished and the last button sewed on: the butler himself carried it downstairs and left it on the kitchen table and then went out of the room, but this time the door was left ajar and Mary-Ann and the scullion and the housekeeper and all the other servants crowded outside, in the passage and on the stairs, waiting, waiting. . . .

'I've grown quite attached to the little chap,' the butler declared. But then, as one of the servants whispered, he'd never had to do any of the clearing up after the Brownie.

'He could be very neat and tidy when he liked,' the housekeeper said. But then, as another servant whispered, he didn't like half often enough.

'If he's under a spell it's the only thing we can do—to set him free,' the butler said firmly.

As the last grains of sand trickled from the hour-glass at midnight, once again the Brownie slipped into the kitchen and sat, cross-legged in front of the fire. Presently he heaved a long, deep sigh, and as on the previous night, began to sing his mournful little song:

> Wae's me, wae's me,
> The acorn's not yet
> Fallen from the tree,
> That's to grow the wood,
> That's to make the cradle,
> That's to rock the bairn,

That's to grow the man,
That's to lay me!

When he had finished singing, he sighed again, and getting to his feet, looked wearily round the kitchen. Suddenly the sad, lost look in his eyes vanished and the Brownie's face was transformed into that of a happy and excited child.

'A new suit!' he cried, jumping up and down and clapping his hands together in his delight. 'A new suit for me!' And he leaped on to a chair and bounded on to the table, where he capered about, laughing and turning somersaults and doing handstands. 'A new suit for me in red and green!'

Eagerly he pulled off his worn, drab clothes and put on the holly-green hose and jerkin, the cherry-red cloak and hood, and round and round the table he danced, singing a new song now:

Here's a cloak and there's a hood,
The Cauld Lad of Hylton will do no more good.

'He's happy at last!' Mary-Ann cried excitedly, forgetting to keep her voice down.

Immediately the back door flew open and a great gust of wind blew in, setting all the burnished pots on the walls rattling and jangling, and the Cauld Lad disappeared into the darkness; but the night wind carried to the listeners in the castle the burden of the Brownie's song:

Here's a cloak and there's a hood
The Cauld Lad of Hylton will do no more good.

'Just like a naughty little boy,' the housekeeper said, 'singing away about doing no more good when far oftener the things he did were really naughty. Ah, well! The spell's undone and the little fellow sounded happy enough as he ran away.'

The butler coughed.

'Simon!'

The scullion jumped. So long was it since anyone had called

him anything but 'Hey you!' or just 'Boy!' that he had almost forgotten he had a name.

'Yes, sir?'

'See the tailor tomorrow about a new livery.'

'Yes, sir.' Simon's face lit up.

'And tell him it's for a second footman, who will probably soon be promoted to first footman,' the butler continued.

Simon the Scullion, who was now a second footman and who shortly would be promoted to first footman, found his tongue at last, and turning to Mary-Ann he took her hands in his.

'Although you are an orphan like me, Mary-Ann, there is more love and understanding in you than in anyone else in this castle. It was you who found out that the Cauld Lad was unhappy and you were the only one who was sorry for him. Will you wait for me while I work hard and save up my wages and when I become head footman, will you be my wife?'

And Mary-Ann smiled.

And do you know what she said?

Of course!

She said—'Yes!'

So hard did they work and so good and kind and understanding were they that when the housekeeper and the butler decided to retire, do you know who was appointed in their places?

Of course!

Mary-Ann and Simon. And they lived happily ever after. The Cauld Lad lived happily too, and never came back to trouble Hylton Castle again. Hylton Castle still stands on the banks of the River Wear, not far from Sunderland in County Durham, and people do say that sometimes, of a moonlight night, a blithe figure in cherry red and holly green can be seen singing and dancing by the banks of the river, but what it is that he sings, no one knows: all they can tell is that the song is gay and lilting and sends them on their way very happy and full of strange content.

11

THE WELL OF THE WORLD'S END

Once upon a time, and a very long time ago it was, there lived a King and Queen who had one child, a daughter, whom they both loved dearly.

They fed her on strawberries and cream and honey cakes topped with yellow marzipan; they dressed her in silks and satins and tied back her corn-coloured hair with strings of pearls and amethysts.

'She is the most beautiful Princess in the world,' they said to each other.

And she was.

'She is as good as she is beautiful,' said the King, 'and she always keeps her promises.'

And he was right.

'She loves all people and all creatures,' said the Queen.

'Except frogs,' said the First Lady-in-Waiting.

'I don't care for frogs myself,' said the Queen stiffly.

'No one would expect a Princess to like frogs,' the King added, and he and the Queen rose from their thrones and went out to play with the Princess in the royal garden.

Not long after this, the King and Queen fell ill, and in spite of all the efforts of the Court Physician, the Queen died and the King knew that he had not long to live.

'Who will look after the Princess when I am gone?' he cried.

'I will,' said the First Lady-in-Waiting. 'Make me your New Queen and I will care for her as though she were my own daughter.'

So the King married the First Lady-in-Waiting, kissed the

Princess and told her always to keep her promises, and then he turned his face to the wall and closed his eyes.

When the New Queen heard that the King was dead, she smiled and sent immediately for the Court Dressmaker and the Court Shoemaker and the Court Jeweller, and she ordered for herself twelve new gowns and twelve new pairs of shoes and twelve new jewelled crowns, each more beautiful and costly than the previous one.

'And what shall we make for the Princess?' asked the Shoemaker and the Dressmaker and the Jeweller.

'For the Princess? Nothing at all,' the New Queen answered. 'She has lived in luxury and idleness long enough. Now she must learn to work for a living. Take away her fine clothes and jewels and dress her in coarse linen and send her to the kitchen to scrub the floors and polish the brass and peel the potatoes.'

So it was that the poor little Princess spent her days working in the kitchen while the New Queen feasted and danced in the hall above, but never once did she grumble, and so gentle was she and so hard did she try to do the unaccustomed work that everyone loved her and did all they could to help her.

One day the New Queen came down to the kitchen and looked around her.

'How is the scullery maid that I sent you getting on?' she asked. 'If any of you have any complaints to make about her, tell me now and I'll see that she's well beaten.'

'Complaints?' said the Cook. 'Why, she is the best scullery maid I have ever had. Show her a thing once, and she does it better than I could do it myself.'

'Indeed!' the New Queen said with a frown.

'There's not a thing that I've asked her,' the Cook continued, 'that she couldn't do.'

'*Indeed!*' The New Queen tapped her foot angrily on the floor. 'If you're as clever as all that,' she cried, taking a sieve from the wall and thrusting it into the Princess's hands, 'then go and fill this at the Well of the World's End, and don't come back until it's full to the brim.'

'Where is the Well of the World's End?' the Princess asked.

'Find out, seeing that you're so clever,' the New Queen cried, and with a triumphant laugh she swept out of the kitchen. 'And that's the last I'll see of her,' she said to herself.

Hopefully the Princess set off with her sieve. But no one in the Palace had heard of the Well of the World's End, and no one in the streets of the royal city knew of it. Through the city gate the Princess walked and out into the countryside, but no one working in the fields had heard of the Well of the World's End, and no merchants or travellers from far-away places knew of it.

Hope gave way to despair as the Princess grew tired and foot-sore, and at last she sank down by the roadside and burst into tears.

'Crying won't get you anywhere,' a shrill voice cried.

Looking up in surprise, the Princess saw an Old Woman, bent under the weight of the logs she was carrying, staring at her with beady eyes.

'Walking hasn't got me anywhere and asking hasn't got me anywhere, so there's nothing left for me to do but cry,' the Princess said.

'There's plenty left for you to do,' the Old Woman said sharply. 'You could carry these logs home for me, to begin with.'

'Certainly,' the Princess said, and picking up the bundle of logs, she balanced her sieve on the top and followed the Old Woman to her cottage.

'I don't suppose you happen to know where the Well of the World's End is?' she said, handing over the logs.

'Then you suppose wrong,' the Old Woman snapped.

First right and over the stile,
Across the river and walk a mile;
Over the hill and through the dell
And across the meadow to the World's End Well.

III

And she went in and slammed shut the door before the Princess could thank her.

'How strange,' the Princess thought, looking at the closed door, and then, forgetting how tired and footsore she had been, she picked up her long skirts in her right hand, and clutching the sieve in her left hand, she ran as fast as she could along the path to the right of the cottage. Soon she came to a wooden stile, and shortly after that she reached a grey stone bridge which arched across a fast-flowing river. Once she started to climb the steep and stony hill on the opposite side, her progress became slower and slower, but when she finally reached the top, she laughed and began to run down the opposite side and on through a valley thick with bluebells, to a wide, green meadow speckled with buttercups and white daisies; through the meadow trickled a little stream, its banks fringed with forget-me-nots and lords and ladies, and the Princess followed this stream to the far side of the meadow until at last she came to the Well of the World's End.

With a little sigh of thankfulness, she sat on the low stone wall which surrounded the well and leaning over, she dipped her sieve into the blue, blue water, but when she lifted it up, all the water ran out. Again and again she plunged the sieve into the water and again and again the water ran out, until in the end the Princess dropped the sieve on the ground beside her and began to weep.

'Isn't there enough water in the well without your having to add to it with your weeping?' a harsh voice asked. The Princess stopped crying and looked around her in surprise, but all she could see was a large Green Frog sitting on the wall at the far side of the well.

'Was that you who spoke?' she asked, drawing back a little because she never had liked frogs very much.

'It was. I wanted to know if there wasn't enough water in the well without your having to add to it with your weeping.'

'You would weep too if you had travelled as far as I have to the Well of the World's End, only to find that the water won't stay in a sieve,' the Princess answered, beginning to cry again.

'Is that all that's worrying you?' the Green Frog asked scornfully. 'Why, I can tell you how to fill your sieve and keep it full.'

'Dear, kind Frog,' the Princess cried, clapping her hands together. 'Please tell me how at once.'

'Only if you'll promise to do whatever I say for one whole night.'

'I'll promise anything if you'll show me how to keep my sieve full,' the Princess answered recklessly.

'Good,' the Green Frog said.

> Stop it with moss and daub it with clay
> And then it will carry the water away.

He gave a little hop.

'Don't forget'—and he gave a little skip—'your promise!' And he jumped back into the Well of the World's End and disappeared beneath the blue, blue water.

Quickly the Princess gathered moss from the side of the well and lined her sieve with it; over the moss she packed clay from the bank of the little stream and when she dipped the sieve in the well it remained full to the brim, and although she ran all the way home—through the meadow and along the dell and over the hill and across the river and over the stile and back to the highway which led to the royal city—not one single drop of water was spilt.

Now, when the New Queen looked out of her window to see the Princess returning, her sieve full of water from the Well of the World's End, she was terribly angry because she thought she had got rid of the Princess for good.

'Tomorrow I must find something quite impossible for her to do,' she thought, and then hiding her anger, she went downstairs to welcome home the Princess.

A little later, just when they were sitting down to supper, there came the sound of tapping on the Palace door, and before anyone could see who it was, a harsh voice outside cried,

> Open the door, my hinny, my heart,
> Open the door, my own darling,
> Mind you the words that you and I spoke,
> Down in the meadow, at the World's End Well.

'Don't open the door!' the Princess cried, growing pale as she recognized the harsh voice and recalled the promise she had given down at the Well. 'It's probably just a beggar.'

'Of course we must open the door,' the New Queen said, noticing how frightened the Princess was. Hurrying to the door herself, she opened it a little; immediately the Green Frog jumped in and hopped across the floor to the chair where the Princess was sitting.

> Lift me to your knee, my hinny, my heart,
> Lift me to your knee, my own darling.
> Mind you the words that you and I spoke,
> Down in the meadow, at the World's End Well.

'Lift you on my knee, Green Frog?' the Princess cried with a shudder. 'I couldn't. Oh, please go back to your home in the Well of the World's End at once.'

'A promise is a promise,' the New Queen said with a cruel smile. 'Do what the creature bids you.'

The Princess hesitated.

And sighed.

Then she bent down and, picking up the Frog with her thumb and one finger, she placed it on her knee.

> Give me some supper, my hinny, my heart,
> Give me some supper, my own darling.
> Mind you the words that you and I spoke,
> Down in the meadow, at the World's End Well.

'Give you some of my supper, Green Frog?' the Princess cried with a shudder. 'I couldn't. Oh, please go back to your own supper in the Well of the World's End at once.'

'A promise is a promise,' the New Queen said, with a cruel smile. 'Do what the creature bids you.'

The Princess hesitated.

And sighed.

Then she picked up her spoon and fed the Green Frog with bread and milk from her own bowl.

When he had eaten all that he wanted, the Frog looked up at the Princess, yawned loudly and said,

Take me to bed, my hinny, my heart,
Take me to bed, my own darling.
Mind you the words that you and I spoke,
Down in the meadow, at the World's End Well.

'Take you to bed, Green Frog?' the Princess cried with a shudder. 'I couldn't. Oh, please go back to your own bed in the Well of the World's End.'

'A promise is a promise,' the New Queen said with a cruel smile. 'Do what the creature bids you.'

The Princess hesitated.

And sighed.

Then she picked up the Frog between her finger and thumb, carried it upstairs and placed it on the pillow as far away from her as was possible. For a moment, the creature looked at her with sad, sad eyes, and then he crouched low against the wall and went to sleep, and as she had had a very tiring day, the Princess curled up and fell fast asleep too.

When she awoke the next morning, the Frog was sitting on the pillow beside the wall, just where she had thrown him the previous night, but if his eyes had been sad then, they were a hundred times sadder now.

Chop off my head, my hinny, my dear,

he said,

Chop off my head, my own darling.

'Chop off your head?' the Princess cried in horror. 'Oh, I couldn't. I couldn't. Even though I've never liked frogs, I couldn't do that to you.'

Mind you the words that you and I spoke,
Down in the meadow at the World's End Well,

the Frog begged.

'Oh, I couldn't. I couldn't,' the Princess repeated. 'You have never done me any harm, and when I was in trouble you helped me.'

Chop off my head, my hinny, my heart,
Chop off my head, my own darling.
Mind you the words that you and I spoke,
Down in the meadow at the World's End Well,

the Frog said beseechingly, and if before his eyes had been a hundred times sadder than the previous night, now they were a thousand times sadder than that.

'A promise is a promise,' the Princess reminded herself. Slowly she picked up the little jewelled knife she used to pare the skin from apples, but the very moment the blade touched the neck of the Green Frog, the creature vanished—and in its place there stood a smiling, handsome Prince dressed in sage-green velvet.

'Thank you for keeping your promise,' he said, bowing to the Princess and kissing her hand. 'You have undone the spell cast on me by an old witch who quarrelled with my father.'

'A promise is a promise,' the Princess said, 'although some are more difficult to keep than others.' And she fell in love with him on the spot.

As the Prince had fallen in love with her when he was still a Green Frog and had first seen her weeping by the side of the

Well of the World's End, they decided to announce their betrothal straight away and to be married on Midsummer's Day.

When the wicked Queen heard what had happened she packed her twelve gowns, her twelve pairs of shoes and her twelve jewelled crowns and left the palace by the back staircase, and has never been heard of from that day to this.

As for the Prince and the Princess, when they became King and Queen they ruled the kingdom wisely and well, and they had seven sons whom they dressed in sage-green velvet, and seven daughters whom they fed on strawberries and cream and honey cakes topped with yellow marzipan. Each evening, when the Queen went up to the nursery and asked her seven sons and her seven daughters what story she should tell them before they went to bed, do you know what they asked for? Of course! The story of the Well of the World's End, and the Princess, and the Green Frog who was really a handsome young Prince.

12

JONAS AND THE BOGGART
OF BRIXWORTH

A long time ago, when fairies and giants both good and bad lived in Northamptonshire, there dwelt near Brixworth a poor young farmer called Jonas: he was honest and hard-working, kind and good, but even his mother agreed that he was not very clever.

'There is no need to worry, Jonas,' she said firmly. 'To be honest and hard-working, kind and good, will be enough as long as you marry a clever wife. Shall I choose one or will you?'

Jonas decided that he would like to choose his own wife, and so the next Saturday he went into Brixworth and looked at the village girls. Some were pretty and idle, caring only for decking themselves in gay clothes and gossiping and dancing on the village green; others were plain and hard-working but did not seem to have a word to say for themselves, but Maisie, the dairymaid at Church Farm, was pretty and hard-working and clever as well, and when Jonas asked her if she would marry him she smiled and said 'Yes', because although he was poor and not very clever, she knew that he was honest and hard-working and kind and good.

With Maisie to help him in the dairy and in the fields, Jonas began to make a little money, which he gave to Maisie, who put it in an old stocking which she hid under their mattress.

A year later, when their first child was born, Maisie took the old stocking from underneath the mattress, emptied out all the money, and gave it back to Jonas.

'Now that you have a son, you must begin to build up the farm and become rich and successful,' she said. 'To do this, you will have to buy more land. Yesterday I heard Widow Peacock say that her nephew has too much land and that he would willingly part with Goosepasture Field, which is separated by the stream from the rest of their farm. Go to him this morning and tell him that if he has a mind to sell, you have a mind to buy, provided that you can both agree on a fair price.'

Jonas took the money and went across to Widow Peacock's nephew, and the two men agreed on a fair price so that by nightfall Jonas was the new owner of Goosepasture Field.

'Good!' Maisie said, when Jonas returned home to the farm that night and told her what he had done. 'Now you must cultivate Goosepasture for three years, and with the money we make on the crops, you should have enough to buy another field.'

The next morning Jonas set to work to plough his new ground, well pleased with himself and with Maisie, his clever wife: all week he worked hard, and it was just as he was turning into the last furrow that he saw a huge, shambling creature, half man and half beast, covered with long, shaggy hair, staring at him with hard little eyes. Immediately—because his mother had told him about such creatures when he was a boy—he knew that this was a kind of giant called a Boggart, and he knew that as well as being very strong, it was cunning and cruel and mean.

'Good day, Boggart,' he said, because his mother had taught him that politeness costs nothing.

The Boggart scowled.

'Goosepasture is my field!' he shouted. 'When you've finished ploughing you can get off it and leave it to me.' And he snarled at Jonas and disappeared.

'Oh, dear!' Jonas said to himself, and as soon as he'd finished ploughing he hurried home to his wife to tell her what had happened.

Maisie rocked the baby in its cradle while she thought.

'Go back to Goosepasture tomorrow,' she said at length, 'and when the Boggart appears, tell him that you bought the field from

Widow Peacock's nephew, and that you're ready to go to law to prove it's yours.'

The next morning the Boggart was waiting for Jonas, grinning maliciously as he looked at the rich, brown earth of the newly ploughed field which he hoped to frighten Jonas into giving up.

'Goosepasture is mine,' Jonas said stoutly. 'I bought it from Widow Peacock's nephew and I'm ready to go to law to prove it.'

The Boggart stopped grinning, scratched his head and scowled at Jonas.

'I hate lawyers,' he said. 'Only a fool goes to them, because they always end up with everyone's money in their own pockets. I'll tell you what we'll do. We'll go shares. That's a good idea, eh? We'll halve the crop between us.'

'I'll think it over,' Jonas promised. 'Come back here tomorrow and I'll give you my answer.'

That evening he told Maisie what had happened and she rocked the baby in its cradle while she thought.

'Tell him you agree,' she said at length. 'Then ask him which he wants—what grows above the ground, or what grows below the ground; and tell him that whatever he decides, he must stick to.'

The next morning the Boggart was waiting for Jonas, grinning maliciously as he looked at the rich, brown earth of the newly ploughed field and thought of the crop he hoped to cheat Jonas out of.

'I'm quite willing to go shares,' Jonas said, 'but there's one thing we must settle first, and when we've settled it, we must stick to it. Will you take what grows above the ground or what grows below the ground?'

The Boggart scratched his head, narrowed his little black eyes and studied the field.

'I'll take what grows above the ground,' he answered at last, 'and I'll come back in the autumn and collect it when you've done all the work.'

'And he shall have what grows above the ground,' Maisie agreed, when Jonas returned home that night and told her all that had happened. 'This year you must plant potatoes in Goosepasture.'

Jonas did as Maisie advised, earthing up when the first green leaves showed and hoeing carefully between the rows, and then he waited until the autumn and lifted the finest crop of potatoes he had ever grown, and just as he was forking out the last plant, the Boggart appeared, bigger and hairier and stronger than ever.

'I've come for my share,' he said, grinning maliciously.

'Certainly,' Jonas answered politely, because his mother had taught him that politeness costs nothing. 'Help yourself. Everything that grew above the ground is yours—weeds and twitch and potato tops. As for me, I'm quite content with the potatoes themselves.'

The Boggart stopped grinning, scratched his head and scowled as he stared from the potatoes, so smooth and large and free from disease and blemish, to the dry withered tops and the weeds and the matted grass which were his share, but he could see no way round the agreement.

'All right,' he growled at last, 'but next year we'll swap, and I'll have what grows below the ground and you can have everything that grows above, and I'll come back and collect my share when you've done all the work.'

'And he shall have what grows below the ground,' Maisie agreed, when Jonas returned home that night and told her all that had happened. 'But next year you must plant wheat in Goosepasture.'

Jonas did as Maisie advised, and he ploughed the field and sowed it with wheat and harrowed it; and when it came time to harvest it, he had the finest field of wheat he had ever grown. Just as he was cutting the last corner, the Boggart appeared, bigger and hairier and stronger than ever.

'I've come for my share,' he said, grinning maliciously.

'Certainly,' Jonas answered politely, because his mother had taught him that politeness costs nothing. 'Help yourself. Everything that grew below the ground is yours—the roots of the stubble and bindweed. As for me, I'm quite content with the corn and the straw.'

The Boggart stopped grinning, scratched his head and scowled as he stared from the corn—so ripe and golden and free from disease—which belonged to Jonas—to the useless roots of the stubble and bindweed which were his share, but he could see no way round the agreement.

'Twice you've managed to get the best of the bargain,' he growled, 'but you won't do it a third time, I promise you! Sow the field with grass next year, and we shall have a mowing match, you and I, and each will take the land he mows.'

'Twice we've outwitted the Boggart,' Jonas said when he returned home that evening and told Maisie all that had happened, 'but next year I am afraid he will steal Goosepasture from us, because he is three times as big as I am and six times as strong, and while I mow a yard, he can mow a rood.'

'No Boggart is going to steal Goosepasture from us,' Maisie said firmly. 'Tomorrow, while I am in the dairy making the butter, I shall think of a plan.'

The next morning she skimmed the cream from the milk and poured it into the churn and she thought hard as she turned the handle of the churn and slowly the cream turned to rich butter: she went on thinking as she drained off the buttermilk and washed the butter and patted it into neat little squares, but when Jonas returned home that evening, she had to admit that she had not managed to think of any way to outwit the wicked Boggart.

'Do not worry,' she said to her husband. 'Tomorrow when I am making my gooseberry preserve, I shall think of a plan.'

The next morning she picked gooseberries from the bushes in the kitchen garden and sat out in the sun while she topped and tailed them and her children played beside her; next she measured the fruit into her big copper pan, added sugar, and hung the pan over the kitchen fire, stirring slowly, and all the time she thought about Goosepasture; but when Jonas returned home that evening she had to admit that she still had not managed to think of any way to outwit the wicked Boggart.

'But do not worry,' she said to her husband. 'Tomorrow when I am spinning wool to weave new clothes for the children, I shall think of a plan.'

The next morning she sat on her wooden stool at the spinning wheel, and she pressed the treadle up and down, up and down, and round and round the wheel flew and the short hairs of carded wool were twisted evenly together and became neat hanks of wool, ready to be dyed and woven into cloth; and a feeling of great content filled her, and quite suddenly she thought of a plan to save Goosepasture from the long arms and great strength of the Boggart.

'Jonas,' she said, when her husband returned home that evening, 'tomorrow you must go down to the forge in Brixworth, and ask Big Steve, the blacksmith, to make you fifty iron rods, all about as thick as the shank of a clay pipe; and before the grass grows green and long next summer and it is time for you to begin mowing in Goosepasture, take those rods and plant them in the half of the field where the Boggart is to start.'

Jonas did as Maisie suggested, and Big Steve made the iron rods, all about as thick as the shank of a clay pipe, and before the grass was green and long in Goosepasture, he took the rods up to the field one night and planted them in the nearer half of the field.

Some weeks later, just as the sun appeared above the horizon, Jonas arose, took down his scythe from the wall of the Great Barn, sharpened it carefully, and set off for Goosepasture. There the Boggart was waiting, bigger and hairier and stronger than ever before, his little eyes gleaming with malice: at the back of the leather belt which he wore round his waist he carried a massive

whetstone, and in his hands there was a scythe three times as big as Jonas's.

'Seeing I got here first, I'll just start in this part of the field,' the Boggart said, hoping to tire Jonas a little by making him walk to the far end of Goosepasture.

'Ready?' he shouted, when at last Jonas reached the far hedge, and without waiting for a reply he swung his mighty scythe and cut through as much grass as it would have taken Jonas quarter of an hour to mow.

'Ha, ha!' the Boggart roared triumphantly, and again he swung his scythe and again he cut as much grass as it would have taken Jonas a quarter of an hour to mow.

'Ho, ho!' he roared, but this time when he swung his scythe the edge caught on the first of the iron bars which was buried in the long, green grass.

'Tough docks you have here,' he muttered, stopping and drawing his massive whetstone from the belt which he wore round his waist, and sharpening his blade with great care.

Again he swung his scythe and again it caught on one of the hidden bars, and again the Boggart had to stop and sharpen the blunted blade on his whetstone. As this happened with every sweep of his great scythe, the Boggart got hotter and hotter and more and more tired and bad-tempered until at last he straightened up and called across the field to the far side where, slowly and steadily, Jonas was mowing the grass so that it fell in neat swathes before him.

'I've never known such a field for docks,' the Boggart cried in despair. 'They're as hard as iron and they're blunting the edge of my scythe so much that before long it will be impossible for me to sharpen it again. What do you say to us having a rest?'

'A rest?' Jonas shouted back in surprise. 'Why, you've hardly started. I'm not going to have a rest until eleven o'clock and it's not eight yet.' And he went on mowing the grass so that it fell in neat swathes before him.

When the Boggart heard this and saw how effortlessly Jonas was mowing his part of the field, he lost his temper completely and threw his scythe down on to the grass.

'Keep your wretched field,' he yelled. 'All it grows is potato tops and wheat roots and docks as hard as iron. I don't want to have anything more to do with it. I'm sick of it—and of you too!'

With a loud cry of rage he disappeared and was never seen again in Northamptonshire. As for Jonas, he smiled happily and went on steadily mowing the grass; but when he returned home that night to tell Maisie that her plan had worked and that Goosepasture was all theirs, he took with him the Boggart's giant scythe, and he hung it up on the wall of the Great Barn beside the place where he hung his own; and people came from far and near to wonder at it—and for all I know, the Boggart's scythe hangs in the barn to this very day.